# LIFT ME, DADDY

Iain Ferguson

Iain Ferguson

Copyright © 2018 Iain Ferguson
All rights reserved.
ISBN: 1721968172
ISBN-13: 9781721968176

# INTRODUCTION

LIFT ME, DADDY has its darkness and its sunshine; has its tears and some laughter. Essentially, it is a tragic love story - the story of a fading Glasgow detective.

The tragedy is the fallout from things that happened to that detective long ago - things having to do with childhood traumas and abuse.

And now, a serial killer has arrived on his patch.

With its beginnings being in the city of Glasgow, the novel's voice can be harsh, sometimes brutal, and the imagery graphic. But as events progress to the Isle of Skye, and back again, the voice softens - but the 'disturbance' remains.

Aficionados of crime fiction, anticipating mystery and the twists and turns of the genre, should be made aware that, although serial killings are a continuous presence throughout the novel, they are fairly routinely solved and, in reality, are almost incidental, their prime purpose being to provide a vehicle by which to convey the novel's principle theme - the detective's life story.

**Cover Design:** *Kenny Ferguson Photography*

## CONTENTS

ONE ............................................................. 1

TWO .......................................................... 23

THREE ....................................................... 35

FOUR ......................................................... 45

FIVE ........................................................... 63

SIX ............................................................. 79

SEVEN ....................................................... 89

EIGHT ...................................................... 117

*And then the beast - the paedophile - satiated and untroubled, rolls away and is almost immediately asleep. But I, the mere child and the beast's victim, do not sleep - cannot sleep! Peaceful slumber is the preserve of the un-hunted.*

*And so I, like other pursued creatures of the night, gaze into the darkness - silently screaming until dawn temporarily releases me.*

# ONE

THE CITY OF GLASGOW. . . EARLY 1980S . . .
'CLOSING TIME' ON A WET AND GUSTY EVENING

The saloon swing doors explode violently open.

The man appears to have been pushed through them, but he hasn't been pushed at all. Being decidedly intoxicated, his rapid mincing gait is merely an attempt at keeping pace with the acute, forward leaning attitude of his body.

Gathering himself to an abrupt halt, a manoeuvre that threatens to reverse the process and propel him back through the doors again, the man is vaguely surprised to find himself in the night.

*Cock---- Bar,* the pulsating scarlet neon sign behind and above him, goes out then - goes out with a haste suggestive of thankful relief. The sign should be saying, *Cockatoo Bar*, but a passing comedian has vandalized the *atoo*.

The rain has stopped.

Well, that's something, supposes the man, some kind of small mercy. It has been raining now, more on than off, for six solid goddamned weeks - doing not a thing for anybody's morale.

The deserted street stretches ahead, dark shadowed and hostile - a canyon of dirty soot engrained tenements. A scatter of multi-coloured squares cling forlornly to the decaying masonry cliffs - coloured squares that are islands of warmth in the impersonal landscape of the city night; symbols of family, of clan, of jealously exclusive human relationships. But, mostly, the squares are black, broken glassed and soulless - eyeless sockets.

Some nights, the realisation that that the majority of the tenements are vandalized and deserted shocks the man. Other nights, the bad nights, he doesn't give a damn. Tonight is proving to be yet another of the latter, one of a recently and increasingly recurring pattern. Tonight, yet again, he has hit the bottle hard - far too hard.

Moving on, he staggers a couple of steps, over-corrects, and focuses his blunted concentration on the task of staying on his feet.

The wind is from the north, bearing the iron bite of Arctic snows and approaching winter; a sneaky prowling wind, prone to apparent sudden death, only to lay in wait and swoop in ambush around canyon corners - buffeting and growling. The man raises the collar of his corduroy jacket against its vindictive spite.

The street surfaces glisten blackly, washed superficially clean by the recent rains, and the city has an uncharacteristic fresh smell. Supposing that that must constitute another small mercy, the man staggers again, overcorrects again, and abandons himself, unconditionally, to the smirking demons of excess alcohol.

A lone car slides past him down the street, a dark gigantic beetle, seemingly un-peopled, silent except for the hiss of rubber on puddled tarmac surface. Stop lights blink momentarily red at an approaching road junction as the beetle turns left and slinks out of sight.

Reaching the junction himself, the man is halted in his tracks by a fresh charge of funneled wind that whips at his clothes and tears at his breath. Another street, another canyon, drifts off at right angles, emptying into a grumbling darkness.

Three youths are fooling and guffawing beneath a streetlamp. They see the man suddenly and the guffawing subsides to an ominous silence. The youths are seeing a middle-aged man, a decidedly drunk middle-aged man. No challenge in that! And by the looks of him, nothing in his pockets worth the picking. The guffawing re-continues and the man staggers on.

Low clouds skim across a disorganised jumble of tenement chimneys, racing swiftly southward, reflecting the bruised glow of the city centre ahead. Somewhere high and remote, in the overhead cliffs, a woman screeches in profane and carnal laughter, and on cue, the eternal city dog barks - anonymous - unseen. Others, further-off, respond: a chain reaction - butterfly barks flitting across the city.

The man staggers wildly again, smiling in reaction - a foolish inward smile at the futile folly that is drunken men. Nearby, a bundle of rags stirs in a darkened shop doorway.

*'Y'orrite Jimmy?'*

The wino's voice is a croak, raucous and raw, not reconcilably human.

*'Y'orrite Jimmy?* (Everything under control James?) repeats the voice, conveying the Glasgow drunks' stock befuddled acknowledgement of passing shadows; the Glasgow drunks' attempted bond of allegiance - a resigned bond of lonely no hope.

The man stops to gaze, compulsively, not really wanting to, at the bundle of rags.

*'Y'orrite Jimmy?'*

The attempted bond, repeated, coils out of the darkness, and a cold chill run through the man. Despite the fogs of his own inebriation, he is recognising dark implications there, furtive comparisons.

A fresh gust of wind howls along the tenement walls, slinks into the doorway and whips the newspaper blankets from the wino's legs, the loose leaves flapping wildly along the pavement, fleeing the night, one leaf clamping around a wet lamp-post and sticking fast.

The man shivers and shuffles quickly on.

Reaching the bridge, he stops to look at the river. Well, what better is there to do - head back to his tenement flat, a dingy one bed-roomed tenement flat? If one knows where to look, one can see it from here on the bridge, in the distance, on the opposite bank, jammed in among a myriad other similar flats in the district called Anderston.

He leans on the parapet and gazes down at the rushing sheet of water, yellow rippling lights reflected in its churning amber currents, debris and discarded rubbish flowing with it.

Raising his head, he sees the source of the yellow lights: beads of naked bulbs strung along the adjoining wharfs and warehouse walls. And all is a dismal, dripping, impotent emptiness. Jesus Christ! Was this what it had come to - the Clyde, the mighty Clyde - an empty hissing husk? The rusted bulk of a moored dredger, yes, but not another ship in sight - the death of a once great world-renowned river.

In times past, how many of his own people, the Gaelic people, had found work in the great shipyards of the Clyde? Or how many of his own people had left their crofts, their mountains and their hearts, fleeing down its iron waters to the four corners of the earth, fleeing its banks forever?

He finds a crumpled cigarette and lights up.

He should have joined his eldest brother Roddy. Had Roddy, in his letters, not said that he should come; that the Highlands were finished sure, that America was the land of milk and honey; that in America were seas of golden corn, waving promises to a man for as far as the eye could see, or the land itself had turned black with cattle?

The man smiles to himself. Och, had Roddy not always been one for the exaggerating? And anyway, the letters had been twenty odd years ago. He hadn't replied - never had been one for the writing of letters.

The cigarette burns itself to a stub, stinging his fingers, and he flicks it over the parapet. The night bays and stirs in the city centre behind him and a sense of desolation seeps into his soul. Remembering the whisky bottle in the kitchen cabinet, and its illusion of comfort, he pushes away from the parapet and staggers north west towards Anderston.

#

The walls of the tenement close are painted in yellow and brown, an overhead light throwing shadows against the peeling plaster finish, the peels hanging like clumps of withered grapes. His flat is on the top floor, four floors up, but stopping at the ground floor landing, prematurely searching for his door keys, he glances at the new woman's door and sees the empty milk bottle - a half pint bottle. And yes, only one! He had noticed that before. Perhaps, like himself, the new woman lives alone?

He wonders if she is already in her bed.

The flat smells damp... musty... familiar. Throwing his keys on the table, he removes his jacket and cloth cap, letting them drop on a chair. In the far wall, a half-drawn curtain semi-conceals a chipped sink and a greasy gas cooker in a small alcove kitchen. Pushing the curtain aside, he finds a glass and the three quarters full whisky bottle and returns to the main room and sits on the sagging moquette couch.

Jesus . . . it's cold!

He rises and lights the gas fire. It burns with a lethargic popping blue flame. Sitting down again, he fills the glass, downs a large swallow and lights another cigarette, vague images drifting towards him through the night from across the river - images of faded rags abandoned in a cold anonymous doorway.

*Y'orrite Jimmy?*

The city hums that indefinable night-time city hum. Every big city seems to have it. He has never been able to determine the source. Phantom generators? Phantom workers at mischievous toil? Perhaps there are sub-cities that ordinary citizens know nothing about?

He draws on the cigarette, downs more whisky and realises that he is hungry. A large greasy fry-up would be nice; but that sounds like too much effort. He remembers reading somewhere that such apathy can be a sign of alcoholism.

He stubs the cigarette and replenishes the whisky.

His aimless gaze wanders to the two framed photographs on the dresser. They are askew. Tomorrow, he must straighten them. Surveying them over the rim of his glass he sees Sarah; broad, dimple cheeked face, auburn hair, generous mouth, tipped up quizzically at the corners; large, honey-brown eyes, the expression vaguely bewildered, rather sad, perhaps reproachful.

He gazes at the photograph absently - or perhaps it is defensively. And just as absently, or defensively, he wonders if she is still with the fellow she had run off with.

His gaze moves to the second photograph, to the youngster that was Angus - a successful doctor in London now by all accounts. Strange that Angus at least hasn't kept in touch.

A dull pain tugs deep in his chest.

He pours yet another whisky, kicks off his shoes and lies on his back on the couch. He downs the whisky in one quick swallow and stares at the pendant ceiling light above him. It is low-powered and baleful. The bulb has burned a hole in the plastic shade. Then the gas runs out, and coldness and grey loneliness settle like roosting bats in the corners of the room. In the draught coming from the window, faded lace curtains faintly flutter, like the lips of an old woman talking in her sleep.

Jesus Christ! Pull yourself together, man. Everything, these days, is doom and gloom - non-stop effin' doom and gloom! Yes, pull yourself together, man!

SOBER UP - GODDAMMIT!

Desolation washes over him in endless choking waves and he feels himself swoon in exhausted surrender.

*Sober up* - he repeats, pleading softly. But already sinking into unconsciousness, he doesn't listen.

The empty glass falls from his hand, clinking against the whisky bottle on the floor, and rolls across the threadbare rug.

#

*Tap. Tap-tap. Tap. Tap-tap-tap.*

The sound is distant, but easing with irritating persistence into the man's sleeping brain. He half wakes and the sound registers; not distant at all but in the room with him - the ivory bead of the blind pull-cord, tapping on the window pane in rhythm with the suck and blow of the rising outside wind. The lace curtains are wildly billowing, the old woman awake now and mouthing silent obscenities. Rain patters and claws at the glass.

He closes his eyes again. He knows what he will see out there, and he doesn't want to see it: another goddamned day, more rain, yet another grey dawn; the same dingy damp-stained walls, yet another futile notch on the monotonous calendar of his life. And yes, apparently, yet another day of self-pity - tiresome self-pity!

A further half hour of fitful sleep and he opens his eyes and sees the overhead light, still lit, glaring accusingly through the melted hole in the plastic shade.

God Almighty, his head is throbbing! The swollen bulk of his tongue feels dry and furred, tastes foul. He swings his legs from the couch to the floor and sinks his face in his hands. Spreading his fingers, he peers at the whisky bottle lying on the threadbare rug, a good golden measure still in it.

*A hair of the dog!*

Now, there is a thought.

# LIFT ME, DADDY

He reaches for the bottle and sees the violent shake of his hand. Despite the coldness of the flat, prickles of sweat are welling on his temples. He has been overdoing the whisky more than ever of late. He had better slow down. A hair of the dog though, is still a good idea.

*Y'orrite Jimmy?*

The wino's croaked acknowledgement had followed him to sleep, had ghosted through surreal dreams, is with him yet - the fevered demand of allegiance, the bond of lonely no hope. His reaching hand recoils away from the bottle. He rises to his feet and staggers. Gongs boom in his head. Christ, he is still drunk! He places his hands on the table for support. Through the fog and the stars making wheels in his eyes he sees the dresser. Yes, goddammit, he really must straighten these photographs - sometime.

The gong-booms subside to a continuous hum and he moves to the window. It is raining cats and dogs, the city strangely empty. Ageing masonry cliffs nudge shoulder to shoulder with younger higher cliffs of steel and glass as far as the eye can see, their sharp-edged heads looming over a blanket of rain-mist and blue smoke haze. A liquid sheet of gunmetal grey slides across a gap in the cliffs, its smooth surface pock-marked by the lash of the rain. The mighty Clyde. Yes, empty! Not a ship in sight!

Down in the street, paper and sodden rusted leaves litter the gutters.

*Autumn!*

Bells begin to peel from the steeple of the church on the corner. He had forgotten it was Sunday. For some reason, Sundays have always depressed him, as far back as he can remember

*Sunday! Autumn! Shit!*

He finds a cigarette, lights up and draws on it ruefully and returns his gaze to the street. A milk float is rounding a tenement corner, a dripping boy running alongside, exchanging empty bottles for full ones in metal crates. It makes him think of the new woman in the ground floor flat. He wonders if she has risen yet.

And then he remembers that he is hungry and has no ten pences for the gas.

#

The man pushes through the door of the corner shop and somewhere a bell twitters - twitters twice - once when the door opens and again when it closes. Ali Khan, a silver haired handsome man looks up towards him, smiling broadly. But Ali Khan is always smiling broadly - nothing new in that.

'Ah! Mr Morrison. How very, very nice to be seeing you. Oh, but dearie me, what a terrible weather. Dearie, dearie me, six whole weeks now and the rain he don't think to be stopping.'

'Aye Ali, I don't know why you ever left Pakistan for this place, far less stay in it this long. You must have made enough money out of the infidels by now to retire back to the heat.'

Ali Khan continues to smile and waggles his finger in the air. 'Oh, you are a terrible teasing gentleman, Mr Morrison.'

'Well, it's nice knowing I'm a gentleman at least. There are some as wouldn't agree with you there. But anyway Ali, let's be having some of your wares……I'll have half a dozen rolls, a packet of sausages, a tin of beans, a Sunday Post - and yes, I'll be having some ten pences in my change…..can you manage all that?'

'Oh, most certainly, Mr Morrison. I am certainly managing all of that.'

'Thank God for Pakistanis and their corner shops, Ali; toiling from dawn until midnight, while our lot lie in their beds…scratching and farting and things…and fuming their outrage at the money being made by Pakistanis. Yes, our feckless lazy lot had better pull their socks up; their Pakistani and Indian neighbours, industrious and determined, could teach them how to get along in life.'

Ali Khan waggles his finger indulgently in the air again, collects the requested items and bags them, having added an extra roll. Not only is Ali Khan a handsome smiling man, he is also a kindly soft-hearted man, invariably adding 'something extra' to the shopping of his elderly or more regular customers.

Mr Morrison glances through the window. 'Looks like the rain is easing at last, Ali.'

'Allah be praised! That will be two pounds and twenty-eight Mr Morrison.' Ali Khan takes the offered five pound note and returns with ten pences in the change. On his way towards the door, Mr Morrison turns and calls over his shoulder:

'Thanks Ali. You take care of yourself now.'

'And you too, Mr Morrison. The blessings of Allah be showered upon you.'

'Och aye, while you're at it Ali, you might put a good word in for me, with the Big Man.'

The bell twitters twice again as the door opens and closes and Mr Morrison disappears into the street. And Ali Khan continues to smile broadly and continues to waggle his finger in the air.

'Oh yes, a terrible teasing gentleman, Mr Morrison,' he informs the empty shop.


The rain has stopped and Mr Morrison breathes deeply at the clean dirty air in an attempt at easing the gongs still booming in his head.

Music is blaring, far too loudly, from a high tenement window - '*Stop yer ticklin' Jock'*. Some deaf sentimentalist is a fan of the Alexander Brothers.

An aroma of frying bacon, meantime, has pervaded the Sunday morning streets, and Mr Morrison decides on the long way home; he has to get some exercise, really must get into some kind of shape again.

A youth and the current love of his life are approaching him along the pavement, arms around waists, pulling each other close - eyes only for one another. He and they are the only humans on the street. Expressions over the moon, they brush past him, unaware that he is there. He doesn't exist.

He arrives at the new glass-walled four-star hotel - *The Crystal Tower*.

Four-star? In Anderston! The world is going mad! At the main entrance, a middle aged uncomfortable looking doorman stands idle beside the polished smoked glass doors. He is dressed in a chocolate brown claw-hammer coat with cute lemon piping, chocolate brown trousers to match, white gloves and a silk top hat.

It is obvious to Mr Morrison that the poor man is feeling rather daft,

Iain Ferguson

but what alternative does the poor man have? He has grocery bills and rent to pay. People might not know it, but he also has a work-shy wife with a lust for 'designer label' shoes and, as a result, a violent interest in his wallet. Forgetting the sleepless nights, all these things mean money! And jobs for men of his age are hard to come by these days. The inflamed, deeply purple veined extremities of the doorman's nose suggest that he has a drink problem - and no wonder!

Mr Morrison knows that it isn't really funny - nor is it polite(!) - to laugh at the predicaments and discomfitures of fellow mortals, but sometimes one can't help oneself - especially when the repercussions are clearly reflected in the shell-shocked expressions on the victims' faces: *what the hell happened!... how the devil has it come to this!* The doorman has such an expression at that very moment, but seeing the approaching Mr Morrison, the expression changes to one that says, *be amused at your peril!*

Amused, Mr Morrison averts his eyes, finds a handkerchief to smother his face and mock blow his nose as he passes the unfortunate man by.

In reality, Mr Morrison is not a man short of an innate sense of humour, but amusement has been a commodity of some great scarcity in his recent life.

Quickening his step now, his smile broadens, and he tells himself that 'that is a lot better. Seeing the lighter side of things again, eh?' Life, of late, has all been doom and gloom - non-stop; cynicism in everything he sees. He has emerging health worries, admittedly, and there is loneliness and no doubt too much alcohol, but that doesn't justify the growing cynicism in his life, the emergent bitterness - the self-pity. Yes indeed, it is time he pulled himself together, time he got his life back into shape.

Approaching his flat and seeing the black car parked outside the tenement close, he recognizes it as an unmarked police car.

Fumbling prematurely for his flat's keys as usual, he notices that the new woman's empty milk bottle has been replaced by a full one - again, a half pint one. And yes, again only one! He hasn't spoken to the new woman yet, but they have exchanged brief smiles in the passing. He likes her smile very much - a broad warm smile that lights up her entire face. Finding his keys, he decides that she will no doubt be up and about by now.

He meets them descending the stairs from the second-floor landing. Detective inspector MacLeod he knows, the younger detective he doesn't.

'Och Willie, just the man. Where the hell have you been at all?' MacLeod's face cracks in a grin. 'Got a wee woman hidden away, is that it now? Well, well you are the dark one.'

Willie's eyes survey McLeod calmly, move to the younger man and back again.

'A fine lot of good a wee woman will be doing me these days.' There is a moment of silence. 'What could it be that you'll be wanting, Ewan?'

'Can we come up, Willie?'

Willie pushes past them. 'If that's what you're wanting.'

The detectives follow him up to the flat.

'Sit yourselves down. I'll put some money in the meter. You'll be having a cup of tea?'

Passing the dresser, inspector MacLeod instinctively straightens the two photographs and sits down.

'By the way Willie, this here is detective constable Craig. Alex Craig. Transferred from Southern Division.'

Willie and the young detective exchange greetings. Willie fumbles with the tea caddie.

'Biscuits?'

'Ach no Willie, the tea herself will be just fine.' As the inspector speaks, his foot strikes the almost empty whisky bottle. Glancing down and seeing what it is, he glances quickly away again. 'I had forgotten what a nice wee flat you have here,' he lies.

There is a further silence.

'Well Ewan, let's get to the point. What is it you'll be wanting?'

Inspector MacLeod coughs. 'We could be doing with your help, Willie.'

'I'm on suspension Ewan - remember?'

'There has been another riddle killing.'

Willie has found three cups which he arranges on the coffee table. The inspector and constable Craig exchange quick glances.

'Same killer, you think?'

'Almost without doubt Willie. Same method. Slit throat. From behind. Right to left. Another typed riddle beside the body. That makes four in a row. Looks like we have a serial killer on our hands. Big flap on now to catch him - and quickly!'

'But Skye is Highland region. Is there some new link with Strathclyde Region that gets us involved? And anyway, I'm on suspension Ewan, so how can I help?'

'The latest murder wasn't on Skye. He has moved to Glasgow Willie. As for the suspension, friends in high up places have spoken for you. It has been reduced, you are back in business as from now. Your appeal against the demotion was rejected, I'm afraid. We tried our best. We are all sincerely sorry Willie. So near your pension and all. Sergeant to constable…makes a big difference. But you left them no choice Willie . . . drinking on duty . . . and not for the first time. You know that yourself.'

The inspector glances towards his companion. 'Alex here is aware of the situation Willie, I'm not breaching any confidentiality. Och no Willie, you left them no choice man.'

Willie's grin is wry. 'I guess I didn't at that.' He finds a cigarette.

'Nationality of the victim?'

'English again. Apparently well-off. But a woman this time.'

'A woman? The English and well-off parts are consistent - but a woman. And in Glasgow you say? Well, that does put a new slant on things. And the letter of signature this time? To date, we have had C, L and O, as I remember.'

'K'

'K? . . . Um, and a riddle?'

'Yes.'

'Ending with, *more to come*'?

'Afraid so, Willie. A riddle and yes, a threat of *more to come.*'

Willie glances across the flame of his match towards constable Craig.

'From your accent Alex, I would be suspecting that you weren't having the Gaelic?'

'Correct Willie, I'm a Glasgow man masel'.'

Willie throws the match in the ashtray.

Craig has found a magazine jammed in the armrest of his chair. 'Ah! So you like motorcycles, Willie? I'm into them big time masel. You own one?'

'No, Alex – well, yes, a hundred years ago! Just like to keep up to date these days.'

Ewan joins in. 'He used to race the dirty dangerous things. Oh aye, Alex, Willie here was a bit of a lad in his day, believe me'

Alex Craig smiles and opens the magazine. Willie turns to inspector MacLeod.

'So, in Glasgow you say Ewan? Three killings on Skye and now one in Glasgow. And by the same killer, it would appear. And a woman. Yes, it sure puts a new slant on things.' He rises and moves to the window.

The rain has returned, but only to a soft drizzle, a grey veil of apathy still draping the city. People are spilling from the church on the corner, families mostly, dressed in their respectful Sunday best - so many people still believing in it all!

Inspector MacLeod arrives by his side and follows his gaze through the window. When he speaks, it's in the Gaelic language.

'All these good people Willie. It's a gladdening sight, is it not? It means that there is still hope. And decent God-fearing people need hope in these violent times. Immorality. Greed. Violence. Society is rotting, falling apart at the seams.' The Inspector glances briefly at the fellow Gael, fellow Islander and long-time friend by his side. 'It's a jungle out there Willie. You and I know that. The world is going to the dogs. It's the men of violence - the little thugs - rule the roost nowadays.'

Willie draws long on his cigarette.

'You know, Ewan, every day as I walk the streets of Glasgow, I see more and more homeless people scattered about in cold doorways. They are invariably alcoholics and the drug addicted. And the ironic thing is, they are so often innately intelligent sensitive good people who simply had bad luck, or couldn't take the strain, surrounded as they are by unjust privilege, indifference and greed. Their life is a dead end - *this is it!* - a life condemned to nothing. All they can dream of is of managing another few steps along the road; of kicking the can a little bit further - of living another day. We all have a desire and a right to bask in and reach for the sun, but because of personal barriers, some among us are denied that right.'

'I'm not talking about these poor souls, Willie - the hopeless drunks and druggies. It's the men of violence and theft, the lawless, the little thugs, I talk about.'

'Perhaps your little thugs are thugs because they have nothing to trade their violence for. We don't like to hear it or believe it, but all of us are born with the potential for violence, Ewan. We are all potential thugs at heart. Thugs are everywhere. Under different guises. There are big thugs - the protected and privileged. And there are little thugs - the unprotected and underprivileged. Some would claim that police work has the potential for thuggery to manifest itself - the power and the abuse of the uniform! And perhaps Ewan, they might just be right at that.'

'Will you no behave yourself man and talk some sense!' MacLeod sounds distinctly indignant.

'There is only a very fine line Ewan, between your little thug out there and your politicians and big money interests - the large corporate criminals, the corporate thugs. All are motivated by power and greed - by survival! Only difference is, coming at the end of the pecking order, your little thug out there is denied the smoke screens of manufactured and legalised justification. That's where you will find the rot in your society Ewan; in hypocrisy, in differing standards of justice - in pecking orders.'

Willie pauses to draw on the last of his cigarette.

'Your little thug Ewan, all of us, if we have any fire in the belly, lustiness of spirit, if we have any salt at all, want to stand high on the pile, want to leave some kind of mark, whether some of us are prepared to admit to it or not, or are indeed even conscious of it. To have gone through life unnoticed or unacknowledged, to have left not even ripples, is an unthinkable thought - is a failed life. Perhaps, in the general terms of pathetic human vanity and of frail human aspirations, it is the fear of no ripples, no justification - no epitaph - that makes your little thug Ewan. And perhaps, in certain hopeless circumstances, thuggery is the only available option that allows a human being his mortal right to say, *"look at me! I am alive - special - take notice!"* And perhaps, and I emphasise *perhaps*, the ones in the same given situation who, being at the lower rungs of poverty and the social ladder and who are afraid to grab that only option, are the defeated, the weak, are the ones who have given up on the possibilities of life, are the ones who are prepared to be devoured by the bigger more fool-proof thuggery of the system.'

It is an agitated inspector MacLeod who glances quickly around towards Alex Craig, thankful on Willie's behalf that the young constable, a dedicated and very enthusiastic policeman, hasn't understood the outrageous Gaelic conversation, and would now appear to be engrossed in the magazine.

'Och, hush with you man! What's wrong with your senses at all? You have been listening far too much to these damned woolly-thinking psychiatrists Willie, and the goody-goody Left. Excuses, excuses. Under-privilege. Bad parents. Slums ….and all the other mumbo jumbo. Well, these self-same slums, self-same parents have produced generations of surgeons, engineers, philosophers, world leaders. And they did it, not by thuggery or by feeling sorry for themselves but by rising up off their backsides and getting on with some honest endeavour!'

'Very true, I agree, but won't you concede that sometimes circumstances, in the lower half of the pecking order in particular, simply won't allow for such good fortune? I am talking about very last available options Ewan, about a choice between being able to say,

*"Look, I am alive!"* and *"Don't bother to look because I don't or hardly exist"*

'No! No! - No Willie! Your thug is perhaps born with a modicum of innocence, but he is also invariably born with a predisposition of becoming a thug. But he has options which will allow him to avoid becoming that thug, or remaining that thug. And if he refuses the right option then the only way to cure him is with discipline, with law and order - the big stick!'

Willie sighs at the same timeworn counter argument.

Y*our thug is born a thug*!

That, in essence, was what Ewan was saying. For a decent educated and frankly a kindly and caring man like Ewan to make such an unconsidered and ridiculous statement defied belief. It was pointless to continue.

The church-goers meantime have dwindled to a few stationary chattering groups. A tousled red headed urchin, the instigator of events, and a young girl with a plastic toy handbag are exchanging rude faces from the smug cover of adjoining adult groups. The contest is being fairly evenly fought until the urchin pulls a face of such flesh defying proportions that the girl intuitively recognises ignominious defeat and, in order to save face, resorts to the role of informant. But gossiping adults being notoriously difficult to distract, the girl's protestations are dismissed, unheard, by an automatic and conciliatory pat on the crown of the head.

Flushed now by success, and with his employment of unsuspecting adult cover being second to none, the urchin feels sufficiently emboldened to produce his coup-de-grace, an exercise that entails a surreptitious pointing of a bony posterior in the adversary's direction, crowned by a derisive slapping of said bony posterior with the hand.

Outraged beyond control and reason, the girl lashes out viciously with her toy handbag only to receive, in return for her efforts, a smack of maternal reproach on her own more rounded posterior, at which final humiliation her face turns scarlet with indignation and the bitter fruits of defeat. To compound her misery, the handbag swipe has missed by a country mile, while the urchin's triumphant face, meantime, peers from behind his own unsuspecting adult group, hand over mouth, purporting to be smothering silent, shoulder-heaving sobs of laughter.

And they will tell you that there is justice in this world!

Willie's sad amusement at the drama in the street is interrupted by inspector MacLeod's voice: 'Ever think of coming back to the fold Willie? As you know, I am West Street Free Church myself. The Reverend Norman McMillan. Excellent Gaelic preacher. A Lewis man. You will be more than welcome, I needn't tell you that. You do, of course, still believe in God, Willie?' There is a tentative anxiousness in his voice.

The defeated little girl, bitterly weeping, has by now buried her crimson face in the depths of her hands and plastic handbag and Willie experiences a pang of impotent pity.

'Believe in God Ewan? I don't know if I do anymore. To tell you the truth, I don't know if I ever really did.' Sensing his friend's shock, he attempts some qualification.

'Perhaps it's religion more than God that I don't believe in. Religion never did make much sense to me. There is inevitably always division. *Them* and *us*. And *us*, of course, are always right. Even our own otherwise close-knit Gaelic community is too often divided by fanatical Catholic and Presbyterian belief. In the process, both sides are taught that that the other side, consisting of their brothers, is wrong, is wicked. That kind of teaching is hate, or can lead too easily to hate. And religion is the greatest teacher of hate on earth Ewan. Oh yes, love of God but hate of those who don't agree with your manner of loving Him. All that matters, surely, is that one believes. All major religions are merely variations of the same theme, variations which most certainly don't warrant the cost of brotherly love. Much of it has to do with political expediency, since it divides and thus weakens and makes troublesome masses more manageable.'

He glances at Ewan and sees him frown silently through the window.

'It's a historical fact,' he continues, 'that religion and its chief exponents, the preachers and holy men, have a great deal to answer for. Just look at your Scottish and Irish Gaelic history and you will see what I mean. Your ministers and priests; one hand pointing their flock towards the emigration ships - *you must go! It is the will of God!* The other hand, meantime, ingratiatingly fondling the arse of the beneficiary - the Saxon laird - old Money Bags up in the Big House.'

'But God, man, you must believe in God! Like myself Willie, your people were fine religious people. You were brought up in the faith. You must believe in God?'

'As I said, Ewan, I don't believe that I do.'

Concern and sadness cloud Ewan McLeod's face. 'Is it because you feel a bit desperate Willie, that you speak like this? Being an old friend, I feel pre-excused for the intrusion of asking, but isn't because of your…eh…trouble that you say such things?'

*Trouble?*

What Willie supposes Ewan means by that is his drink problem, his alcoholism. Why didn't Ewan say it straight? Why was it that people invariably went around the subject? Alcoholism. He himself is concerned by it admittedly, but he is prepared to admit to it. It is only another ailment after all.

'It isn't desperation that I feel Ewan, only a vague apprehension, which is natural enough.'

'In that case, God can help you Willie. All the men I have known in your position have turned to Him in their time of trouble.'

'Well, every man is at liberty to do that if he feels the need. I just don't feel that need.'

Ewan isn't put off. 'If you try Willie, really try, you can overcome your trouble.'

*Trouble* again.

Willie is becoming bored by the conversation but Ewan is beginning to sound vaguely distressed and he feels obliged to pay attention.

'I know only too well Willie, that this little flat is suffused with your loneliness. I am your friend and I know. Every time I visit you here I feel for you. And yet, believe me, I speak from the bottom of my heart; if you believe, truly believe, God will help you.'

An alley cat is braving the puddled surface of the street below. It is now the only living creature in sight. The worshippers have vanished. Victors and vanquished have departed the battlefield of hum-drum human existence.

*- Y'orrite, Jimmy? -*

Willie feels suddenly tired and apathetic. He wishes that Ewan and Alex Craig would depart and leave him with his 'lonesome' little flat.

. . . Alex Craig! He had forgotten about the presence of Alex Craig. The young detective is now idly flicking through the pages of the magazine. His exclusion from the Gaelic conversation has been decidedly bad mannered. But Ewan, it would appear, isn't finished quite yet.

'I'm on your side Willie, remember that. We are from the same people, you and I, from the same township on Skye . . . from the same sound Christian upbringing. I will pray for you.'

Willie feels something give way inside him. Like all deeply religious people, Ewan can be so downright sure of himself. How can he know what is happening, really happening, in a friend's soul? Willie feels like telling him not to waste his confounded prayers on him, but that would be unkind, Ewan means well.

It might appear as if Willie's life is empty but at least he is sure of where he stands, sure of the death that his *trouble* might have determined will be earlier in coming. Perhaps that is all he now has, but that knowledge is something he can get his teeth into. Over recent years he has been trying to establish something of some significance that will justify him, but he has decided that nothing has that much importance anymore. What difference can it really make, the way one decides to live, the fate one thinks one chooses? What difference can it really make to him, Sarah's vanished love or Ewan's God? And what difference can it make if he were to kill himself early with a self-inflicted *trouble*, since it all comes to the same thing in the end - oblivion!

His thoughts are drifting . . .

. . . what did it really matter if Angus hadn't kept in touch?

. . . what did it matter if, at that very moment, Sarah was being screwed by the fellow she had run off with?

. . . what did it matter if, at that very moment, Sarah was being screwed by the postman?

. . . what did it matter, even, if the postman was being screwed by the fellow Sarah had run off with?

. . . or, indeed, vice versa?

What the hell did any of it matter! That was the way the world was.

Listening to the echoes of these thoughts, he gazes apathetically through the window. He is breathing softly, aware of a long silence. The silence is communicating regret, as he tries to recall a time, not that desperately long ago, when he hadn't felt that way at all; to a time when all of these things *had* mattered - had mattered so very much!

His gaze wanders along the street, all the way to the bridge. To go further, it would require to cross the river.

Constable Alex Craig has by now cast the magazine aside and he coughs rather pointedly in the background, the sound intruding upon Willie's thoughts. Reverting to the English language, he speaks.

'The killer's latest note Ewan, what was the riddle this time?'

'Pardon? Oh, . . . yes.' Ewan fumbles for his wallet. 'I have brought you a copy.'

He hands Willie a folded sheet of paper, which is accepted but not looked at.

'Leave it with me Ewan, I will study it later.' He gazes at the grey falling of renewed rain. 'So, they have turned down my appeal against the demotion?'

'Afraid so Willie. As I said we are all very sorry. We did our best for you. But try not to worry about things. In the meantime, we can be doing with your assistance on this case: your long experience of and rapport with the Glasgow underworld, and crucially, the apparent links to our own island of Skye. He could be a Gael Willie. Anyway, we must catch him, and quickly. Alex Craig here has been assigned to assist you; a fresh face from Southern Division and an old hand like yourself should result in a productive combination. And the best of luck to you both. You are going to need it.'

The inspector and constable Craig depart.

The day crawls past and another night sweeps in, and with it yet more loneliness and a renewed urge for liquor. Willie glances at the whisky bottle abandoned under the chair. Yes, a good golden measure still in it.

'Ach, why the hell not?'

Grabbing the bottle, he drains it into a glass and studies the inspector's sheet of paper again, straightening its wrinkles on the table before him.

As with the previous three murders the killer has, along with a riddle, allocated a number and a letter of signature. Added to that is the threat, *more to come* - an ominous portent indeed.

He reads:

*'No 4. To increase the heat, will they need the peat?*

*- more to come!*

*Signed K'*

Well, well, this was a strange affair indeed; a riddle beside every body. He has dealt with killers before, reckons he has some inkling as to their psychology. Many of them crave notoriety, recognition, leave suicidal clues to these ends. In the riddles could be such clues.

*'To increase the heat, will they need the peat?'*

What could be meant? Alternatives to peat? Gas? Oil? Could fire be of significance? Was there more than one killer? Was he indeed a Gael? Three killings out of four in Gaeldom, on Skye, yes, but that proved nothing. Reference to peat though, a predominantly Highland fuel. He rubs his chin, rises to the dresser and retrieves copies of the notes found by the previous three bodies on Skye. These too, he spreads on the tabletop. After each riddle are his own bracketed queries - wild theories - a clutching at straws.

*'No 1. Useful for sleep, but they made us weep!*

*- more to come!*

*Signed L*

(Drugs? Pills? Sheep? Whisky? . . . US!?)

> *'No 2. Not black men, who then?*
>
> *- more to come!*
>
> *Signed O*
>
> *(White men? Brown Men? Yellow men? Red men?)*
>
> *No 3. Twice twenty plus five, so few left alive*
>
> *- more to come!*
>
> *Signed C*
>
> *(45? 1945? World War 2? Some anniversary?)*

And what of the letters of signature which, taken in sequence, said LOCK? All the victims have been English - three men and one woman. What the hell does it all mean? A myriad wild possibilities stir and nudge at the back of his mind.

Glancing up, he sees where Ewan MacLeod has straightened the photographs, and he allows himself a smile.

Another unlikely possibility strikes him and he licks the lead of his pencil - a habit from schooldays - and notes the possibility in his notebook.

He is back at work. He has never considered it the best kind of work a man could engage in. Having been kicked out of The Glasgow School of Art in the mid-fifties, he has often wondered how the pendulum of fate has lead him to police work - prying on, hunting, possibly destroying the lives of fellow men. But right now it is some kind of purpose to life - another small mercy.

The whisky is finished and the *Cockatoo Bar* distantly beckons - but to hell with it meantime.

*- Y'orrite Jimmy?-*

He smiles another smile and licks the pencil again.

# TWO

Detective Constable Alex Craig picks Willie up at 4.00 pm to begin the back shift. Willie, meantime, has arranged for himself and Craig to view the injuries sustained by the latest murder victim, and on their arrival at the city morgue, they find the pathologist awaiting them, ready to perform an autopsy.

Having been in and out of morgues most of his adult life, a hazard that went with the job, Willie has never learned to accept them with any degree of composure or detachment, can never rid himself of a sense of despair - the clinical medical smells, the chill sterile surfaces of tile, marble, stainless steel.

Victim number four lies on her back on the dissecting slab, naked, her thighs and stomach bulging with approaching middle age and well-fed privilege. Large bosoms sag like cold hot water bottles, drooping over her rib cage. Her head is thrust back, filmed unseeing eyes directed at the ceiling. Her hair has been blue rinsed - sad last echoes of normal human vanity - ironic now in its contrast to the blue-tinted death of her skin. She has an aristocratic aquiline face, had been a handsome woman in her day. The label attached to the big toe of her left foot says: *Penelope Madeleine Wainwright, nee Simms.*

The gaping purple gash ripping across her throat is obscene, unreal, gives the corpse the illusion of an oversize mutilated doll. It's hard to imagine that Penelope Madeleine Wainwright, nee Simms, had ever been possessed of life, beating heart, coursing blood, need of love.

The police pathologist pulls on a pair of powdered rubber gloves - just another man preparing for just another job - and Willie experiences a renewed surge of an old resentment; an unreasonable resentment he has long harboured for the license afforded the medical profession over helpless modest fellow mortals; a psychological deep seated thing, with foggy roots he doesn't understand. Medical people - curers, true, but too often arrogant and unaware destroyers of dignity and privacy also.

Looking at the aristocratic dead woman, Willie can picture her, not that very long ago: tea parties, airs and graces, vanities, hopes, fears. Just look at her now! Naked and insensitively exposed…at the mercy of probing fingers, cutting knives.

'As you can see, sergeant Morrison, the victim has had her throat cut, right to left, consistent with the PM reports we received on the three previous victims found on the Isle of Skye. If, as we suspect, but aren't yet certain, the attacks were carried out from the rear, that would suggest that the assailant is left-handed'

Remembering Willie's recent demotion too late, the pathologist glances at him briefly, over horn rimmed spectacles, but having long known and liked Willie, he refrains from correcting his mistake as to his current rank.

'Sexual assault, doctor?'

'Apart from the fact that she was found fully clothed and her clothes undisturbed, as was the case with the three previous victims, there is no evidence to support any sexual interference. Also, all the necessary swabs were taken and tested with the latest technology, and all results proved negative. I will now be investigating the digestive tract and stomach for evidence of the sedating substances discovered in each of the three previous victims.' That said, the pathologist chooses a wicked looking scalpel from a stainless-steel tray of intimidating instruments.

Constable Craig pops a stick of chewing gum into his mouth and surveys the corpse through narrowed eyes: 'Some bush! Eh?' he grunts.

The schoolboy crudeness and brutish insensitivity of the remark registers through incredulous disbelief. Willie and the pathologist imperceptibly stiffen, responding to the profane and inappropriate observation with the silence and non-reaction that it warrants. A wave of weary sadness washes over Willie's soul. As the pathologist inserts the scalpel into the flesh above the corpse's pubic bone, he experiences an onslaught of approaching nausea.

'If at all possible, I would appreciate an advance copy of the autopsy report as soon as it is available doctor. As you are aware, time and speed are of the essence in murder cases. Thank you for your time doctor. Come on Craig, let's go.' He walks briskly towards the door, eager to vacate the cold clinical atmosphere, anxious to be distanced from omnipresent death.

Lying back in the passenger seat of the unmarked car, he draws on a cigarette while Alex Craig drives. The rain has stopped again. A brisk wind has dried the rusted leaves that are increasingly invading the streets, hoisting them from the gutters, and they now rampage in aimless spirals along the city pavements, clawing at walls and pedestrians' legs.

Yes, autumn!

The sun has fallen beyond the city skyline, the pale lemon of its watery setting reflected in the uppermost windows of a high tower block ahead - a beacon of light against the ever darkening sky - while a spreading rash of garish neon is smearing the shadowed depths of the passing canyon floors: Glasgow is applying her whore's make-up, is preparing for yet another night of mayhem and mischief. Alex Craig fumbles in his pocket for a pack of chewing gum, offers Willie a stick.

'No thanks.'

'You said the Gorbals, Willie? Where exactly?'

'Cumberland Street. The Phoenix Bar.'

Alex Craig throws him an intent look. 'The Phoenix? That den of Fenian weasels!'

'Business is business Alex.'

Craig swings the car left into a new canyon. Willie glances at him, sidelong. About thirty, he reckons. Bullet head…neat close-cropped sandy hair…trim moustache….. obviously over-fussy about his appearance….undoubtedly ambitious. The eyes are a nondescript but restless blue grey. He is chewing noisily and open mouthed on his gum. Without doubt, Alex Craig has supreme confidence in himself, is a man who knows he is right - always right. But hadn't also Heinrich Himmler! Willie glances through the side screen. Shadowed canyon after shadowed canyon pass them at right angles.

*Some bush, eh?*

That's all Craig had seen or taken in back there. It hadn't once been a human being at all, but a mere object, an object of derision, a target for unfeeling and obscene self-indulgence. It was being said that television, the media, had much to do with things. Brutalised. Death and violence by the minute. Death meant nothing anymore. Life meant nothing anymore. It had all been reduced to a game. Willie decides he doesn't like Alex Craig. The car slinks into Cumberland Street.

'Pull her in over here.'

'But the Phoenix is two blocks away.'

'You are staying here Alex. I'm going in alone.'

Remembering Willie's *trouble,* Alex Craig looks at him with barely concealed scorn. Willie reads the younger man's suspicions.

'I said it was business Alex. And business it is. You were transferred from Southern Division to this Division because they don't know you as a dick around here.' He hopes that his emphasis on the word *dick* has been un-intentional. 'Let's keep it that way meantime. If they see you with me they will know. Don't worry old chum, you will come into your own soon enough, I can assure you. Keep your eyes open. See what and who you can see. The powers of observation can be crucial in this business. Half an hour should see me through.'

He doesn't say anything, but Alex Craig feels 'put down' and demeaned. And Alex Craig isn't one who likes to be put down or demeaned - by anybody!

The rank odours of the Phoenix Bar, a very old establishment, pervade the street, hit you before you open the swing doors:- stale liquor…cigarette smoke….old sweat. Beyond the doors, the escapes and the depravities of today - dreams and boasts, violence and carnality - rub shoulders with the drifting ghosts that were the identical escapes and depravities of yesterday; an unending human drama, unending human tragedy; an endless repeat performance, staged in a shrine to cobwebbed tears and desperate vanished laughter - petrified warnings unheeded by countless generations.

The Phoenix is also an establishment that makes no concessions to nicety or good taste. The plastered walls are painted a practical but dismal vomit yellow, the ceiling an unashamed spanked bottom scarlet. The linoleum floor is liberally sprinkled with sawdust. There are plastic chairs and formica veneered tables. The main feature of the place is the imposing Victorian oak bar and a huge ornate gantry mirror, over which is hung, in pride of place, a fly-blown photograph of Celtic football team, the proud European Cup winners of 1967 - Britain's first!

The Phoenix is, without doubt, a man's world, the sprinkling of women present defying the dignity of their gender by their presence, their language and the bawdiness of their guffawing raucous laughter. The Phoenix is also a thriving relic of religious bigotry and the old gang wars.

*Glasgow - no mean city!*

Willie pushes to the bar. The wild confusion of voices stills momentarily - a pig, the police, the 'enemy', has arrived! Subjects of discussion are hastily amended; voices lowered a few degrees. The language remains the same, 'fucks' and 'bastards' punctuating the gabble of slurred conversation. The barman stops drying his glasses, slings his dish towel across his shoulder and moves along the bar.

'Hullo therr, Mr Morrison. Lang time no see. Wharr'll it be then?' The barman's eyes, stoic and non-committal, convey no emotion, neither welcome nor rejection.

'Hello Joe. A whisky would be nice. Talisker. Make it a double'.

As Joe moves to the optic, Willie is aware of the devil that has settled on his shoulder - had half expected it! (*What's this! Drinking on duty again? ....*Ah, but this is different. This is not, 'on duty', this is, 'in the line of duty' ..... *But a double whisky? Why not a fruit juice, or a half pint shandy?* . . . Shut up! Go away! To communicate you have to connect.

Joe pushes the glass twice against the optic and Willie glances along the bar.

There are natural born leaders of men, men who stand out, who are different to other men, who are difficult to ignore. There is an aura about them - to do with awe, hero worship, dominance - drawing lesser men around them like moths to a flame.

Edward O'Halleron is such a man. Willie had seen him immediately he had entered the saloon, to the right, at the far end of the oak bar, leaning on his elbows and staring in apparent disinterest at his drink. He is big for a city man, dwarfing the disciple thugs on either side of him. Willie knows that O'Halleron has seen him. The disciples too are studiously surveying their drinks, but all the while giving their 'messiah' muted progress reports from the sides of their mouths. Joe places the whisky on the bar.

'Err ye arr, Mr Morrison.'

'Thanks Joe.'

A brassy tart, with Sumo wrestler legs and a non-existent mini-skirt that is twenty years too young for her, rises from one of the tables and heads for the toilet, bumping against the table of a derelict red nosed drunk. Beneath the tilt of a dirty cloth cap, the drunk's face is slumped on his chest, a loose saliva-soaked mouth muttering non-stop obscenities at an empty wine glass.

'Ah, fuck aff! . . . ya bastard! . . . aye, ye . . . '

Beside him, a toothless crone is cackling with mirth at the antics of the little pink elephant in a frilly ballet frock, pirouetting merrily on the table. Already pie-eyed, the pair of them had arrived at the Phoenix together - a wine soaked two and a half hours before. By now, not only fellow mortals but also physical surroundings are a confusing blur. As far as either of them are now aware, or care, they are perhaps no longer in Glasgow, they could be in Saskatchewan.

The jerk of the table registers in the drunk's reeling senses. Vaguely aware now of other people in the world, his head revolves slowly upwards, a glazed expression endeavouring to catch up with the tart's erratic progress towards the toilet.

'Y'orrite Jimmy?' he rasps at the empty air three feet behind her, his head completing the revolution and slumping back onto his chest. The tart meantime trips through a door that says 'ladies'.

'Jesus wept,' thought Willie, 'ladies indeed!' He moves along the bar towards O'Halleron. 'Hello Ted, mind if I join you?'

O'Halleron feigns surprise. 'Oh! Hullo therr, Mr Morrison. Well, well, huvna seen ye aroon' in a lang time. How's it gawin'?' A disciple thug moves truculently aside and Willie sits down.

'Perhaps I should be asking yourself the same thing Ted. How's it going?'

O'Halleron chuckles 'Well, ye ken me Mr Morrison - a paragot o' virtue.'

'Yea, sure Ted, I *ken* you fine. As you say, a paragot o' virtue. Your glass looks kind of empty. Let me fill her up. As I remember it, *heavy* is your poison?'

O'Halleron drains his dregs. 'Dinna mind if Ah dae. Yer a real gent Mr Morrison, and nae kiddin'.

Willie orders a pint of 'heavy' beer and Joe brings it over. There is a cautious exploratory silence.

'Whispers has it that ye hud a spot o' trubble Mr Morrison - demoshun! Too much o' tha old John Barleycorn, eh?' That observation makes it one up for Ted O'Halleron, puts him on the front foot. He throws Willie a gorgeous grin. 'But don't we all hiv oor trubbles, eh?' He raises his glass. 'Here's mud in yer eye Mr Morrison.'

Willie smiles cynically to himself in the gantry mirror. News sure travels fast in the underworld. There is another silence.

'No doubt you heard about the murder, Ted? The woman in Kelvingrove Park?'

'Read aboot it in ra papers Mr Morrison. Sure as hell did. Whit's ra wurld comin' tae Mr Morrison?'

'People have no respect for the law anymore. That's what the world is coming to Ted.'

O'Halleron surveys him earnestly and tut-tuts. 'Ah guess that's whit it is Mr Morrison. Terruble, so it is. Jus' terruble!' He throws Willie another gorgeous grin. 'As ye says, Mr Morrison, nae respect any mair, nae respect for onything! The wurld is gawin' tae the dugs! Take, fur example, aw they poofs that is movin' in. Mair and mair poofs movin' intae Glesca every day. Everywherr ye looks - poofs! Ah reckon it's an Edinburra conspiracy masel'. Edinburra always wus full o' pansies. Noo they is sendin' their pansy overspill tae Glesca!'

'You reckon, Ted?'

'Oh aye! Nae doot aboot it. Glesca's an awfy daingerus city nooadays, Mr Morrison. A daicent man is afraid tae go tae sleep in Glesca nooadays, in case he wakes up in tha mornin' wi a limp condum hangin' oot his erse.'

The imagery is obscene, intentionally vulgar and brutal, meant to shock. A disciple tries not to choke on his beer, but doesn't quite make it. Willie himself has difficulty keeping a straight face. Sipping at his whisky, he glances at this notorious and dangerous hoodlum by his side. He sees the battle scars, the alert pale blue eyes, the firm determined jaw; a big handsome man with coal black hair - a feared fighting man. But there, also, is keen intelligence, and he thinks, 'what a waste' There, had the right doors been open, is a dynamic board director, a successful politician; perhaps a movie star, an artist, a poet - anything he wished to be.

But the right doors, for Edward O'Halleron, have been tightly closed in his face and firmly bolted. Accidents of geography and social circumstance have predetermined Edward O'Halleron's allocated station in life; unless he is lucky, near the foot of the pile. But Edward O'Halleron is not one to accept predetermination or to trust his fate to luck, is not one to let such drawbacks stand in his way. Oh no! - Edward O'Halleron will scramble to the very top of any pile that presents itself. Life is short and, by Christ, life is only what you yourself make of it. You can be a shrinking violet or you can be a god. The choice is in your own hands. And if the only doors available lead outside of the law, well, you burst through them and announce that you are alive - something special - and to hell with the bastards!

Willie takes another sip of his drink and thinks of Ewan MacLeod; *thugs are born thugs!*

'The woman in Kelvingrove, Ted. What I'm saying, if you hear any more of these whispers of yours....'

'Ah hears ye loud and clear Mr Morrison.' O'Halleron taps the side of his nose in a knowing and confidential gesture.

Willie drains his glass and makes to move away. O'Halleron grabs his arm. 'Ma bruther Liam, Mr Morrison. Spot o' trubble ye ken. Breakin' and enterin'. His case comes up a week Wednesday. One good turn an' aw' that?'

'No promises Ted. I'll see what I can do. Depending on the whispers of course.' Willie moves to the door, the draught of his passing stirring the stupor of the red nosed drunk.

'Y'orrite Jimmy?' rasps the red nosed drunk.

Beside him, the crone has fresh tears of mirth streaming down her cheeks, and is cackling anew.

The little pink elephant is getting out of hand.


Willie slides into the car. Alex Craig's earlier annoyance at being left behind has been simmering, rising to a seething resentment and making his blood boil. Throwing his magazine into the back seat, he pulls away from the kerb.

'Where now, then?'

'Let's see the other side Alex. Bridgeton. The King George Bar. Let's hear what the Protestants have to say for themselves.'

Night has marched into the city. It has started to rain heavily again and the windscreen wipers slap the neon lights of the canyons in and out of focus, smearing their colours across the screen - a Jackson Pollok abstract. Alex Craig chews noisily on his gum, barely pausing as he enquires: 'Well, how were our criminal Fenian friends then?'

Willie lights a cigarette and glances at him across the flame. 'You don't like Catholics, Alex? They are the bad guys, that it? The Protestants are the good guys, the guys in the white hats - simple as that?'

'Parasites!' A hard glint of bigotry dances on the fire in Alex Craig's eyes. 'Thick as thieves! Stick together, the bastards! Get one in, all in! Close ranks!'

'If I'm not mistaken Alex, that is the age-old Catholic complaint against the Protestants. Funny handshakes. Rolled-up trouser legs. Masons and all that jazz.'

But Alex Craig hasn't heard.

'Glasgow! A Fenian takeover! Of my city! Glasgow corporation, the social services - taken over - a whitewash! Taken over by Irish Catholics,... to be followed soon, the way things are going, by Pakistani Muslins! Ship them all back to where they came from! Foreign bastards! Destroying my city! Destroying my country! Destroying my religion! Irish and Pakistanis - the whole damn fucking

Iain Ferguson

lot of them - OUT!'

'That's a lot of hate, Alex. And covers a lot of ground....what about the Eskimos?'

'Aye...these bastards too!'

Feeling crushed by such bigoted venom and scaremongering rhetoric, Willie remains silent. Alex Craig swings the car violently left, into another canyon.

'Just like your lot, Willie - Gaelic men - bog trotters! *Teuchters*! The Glasgow police force - the promotions, the top jobs - traditionally riddled with *Teuchters*. McLeod. McKay. McDonald. All the fucking Macs of the fucking world. Once in, all in together boys - over and out!'

Willie looks at him in bemused disbelief. 'For God's sake, Alex! Did you shit the bed this morning? Or are you always this cheerful?'

'Oh, don't you go worrying aboot me none, Mr *Mac* Morrison. I have me brains. I will pass the exams. I'll make it to the top, but under my own steam and on merit - so help me!'

An agitated Alex Craig has stopped chewing, his bared teeth clamped tight with emotion on his gum, the jungle lights of the city reflecting in his eyes. Wondering what the hell has brought it all on, Willie glances forlornly through the side screen. Two police cars, their blue lights flashing, are parked in front of a low-class bar while uniformed policemen struggle to contain a wheeling fist fight rampaging along the sidewalk.

'You are a man of many prejudices Alex, not good qualities in a person, especially in a policeman. Do you think they need help?'

'Fuck them, there are six of them, they can manage. And fuck you Morrison! Every man has his prejudices.'

Willie stubs his cigarette, conceding to himself that Alex Craig is right in that - every man had his prejudices. And like every other man, he himself has to have them too. He tries at that moment to determine what they are, but can't. That gives him some amusement.

The car swings into London Road, towards Bridgeton and the King George Bar.

#

He pushes the remains of his fish supper, still wrapped in newspaper, across the table, pours himself a whisky and tries to recap on the day's events.

The 'King George Bar' had been the Protestant counterpart of the Catholic 'Pheonix': Dusty Miller, the Protestant counterpart of Catholic Ted O'Halleron, counterparts that seethed with uncompromising hatred of the other.

Religious bigotry and violence! Gang wars! It was such things had helped give Glasgow its reputation - the terrible side of its reputation. But in the mix also, in perverse contradiction, there was art, culture and creativity and an unparalleled warmth, friendliness and helpfulness – a surprising unlikely mix that had contributed to the city's simmering vitality, its renowned unique humour, its undoubted human colour. You either loved Glasgow or you hated it. There was no shilly shallying on the fence - no half measures.

Yes - *no mean city!*

He reaches for his whisky, Sarah and Angus surveying him in reproachful silence from the dresser. He peers back at them, as he so often does, over the rim of his glass, and slides them from his thoughts which began to drift.

The new woman's milk bottle - still only one - had been empty again, and neatly placed as always by the door of her ground floor flat.

Jesus! - he is lonely.

He straightens the paper wrinkles from the four murder riddles, arrayed among the remains of his supper, and tries to formulate his thoughts, but can't.

*America is the land of milk and honey. You must come. Scotland, the Highlands, is finished* - his brother Roddy's words come to him.

He should have replied. Roddy and he had been so close. But it had all been so long ago. What was Roddy now? A tycoon – a rich and happy man no doubt.

He gulps at the whisky.

And what of Finlay, his favourite uncle? An uncle who is not much older than himself. A committed bachelor. Living alone. Still on Skye, the island he had unbelievably never once left, had never ever had the desire to leave. Finlay, who had never seen a train; inarticulate and uncomfortable in the English language - a language which, he claimed, stuck in his throat. Totally at home only in the Gaelic tongue. Finlay. A relic? Flotsam on the sea of human progress? Progress? A dinosaur is no doubt how Alex Craig would have described him, had he but known of his existence.

He downs his whisky.

- *Y'orrite Jimmy -*

- *Some bush, eh? -*

- *Every man has his prejudices -*

Prejudices! Again, he tries to determine what are his own - he must have them. Again, he can't. He is too good to be true! He laughs out loud, and rather foolishly. He pours himself another large whisky … and then a large last one … and then another large last one … and finally, a last large last one.

He staggers to the bed and falls across it. And sleep - troubled sleep - advances like a black bottomless hole and he tumbles in.

## THREE

It is two days before Christmas and Willie has the day off.

Meantime, there has been another killing. Number five. Like number four, in Glasgow. Again an Englishman. Same method. Another riddle beside the body.

> *No.5 They will sever your tongue, and then you are done!*
>
> *- more to come!*
>
> *Signed T*

And the only significant developments relating to victim number four, the Englishwoman found in Kelvingrove Park, is the discovery that she had links with the Isle of Skye, having once owned a fishing/shooting estate on the island.

Anyway - day off! He will think about it later.

#

The pedestrian precinct in Glasgow's Buchanan Street is thronged by last-minute Christmas shoppers.

A young female busker with an enigmatic face is playing a tenor sax: *I wish I was in Dixie.* Liking the sound and fascinated by the face, Willie sits on a bench to listen. Hovering overhead, strings of coloured decorations - jolly balls and bells - thread back and forth across the street. The sky beyond is low, metallic, visibly moving. Tinsel, holly and over-fed, red faced Santa Clauses on reindeer drawn sledges give a festive atmosphere to shop windows, goading reckless shoppers to a flush of goodwill towards all men.

Two women with headscarves are chatting scandal on the pavement nearby - a battle of tongues - listening but not hearing, their mouths already formulating the continuation of their own more exciting brand of scandal. They are what are patronisingly referred to as 'common women' - in Glasgow parlance, *'wee herries.'* (little hairy women.)

One of the *wee herries* has a child of about six in tow. Scandal doesn't interest him. Bored, he wanders off and gets swept along by the milling throng. His absence registers. The *wee herrie* mother glances up, just in time, and spots him, runs after him, catches him, raises her hand and slaps him hard across the head - out of nowhere. Willie winces at the certainty of the flashing stars exploding in the child's skull. The child's mouth opens in sudden shock; his yells, sticking in his chest, refuse to materialise, then burst forth, sore and uncomprehending.

The *wee herrie* grabs his arm and drags him back to her scandal. The child's screeching spews uncontrollably from the fiery redness of his face, from the gaping black hole that is now his mouth. The *wee herrie* shakes him.

'Ye waant I gie ye another clout, ye wee scunner!' *(You want me to give you another slap, you little brat!)*

The screeching continues unabated - a confused lament at the outrages and injustices of life. A seed has been sown in dark childhood memory. A possible thug in the making? What would Ewan MacLeod have made of it?

The enigmatic busker has just finished playing *Stranger on the shore* and has started on *Rainy night in Georgia.* Willie studies her, increasingly fascinated by her. She has exceedingly high cheekbones and taut olive skin drawn tightly across a finely chiseled face. The sculptured nose has a subtle raptor curve to it. She reminds him of a Peruvian Indian - some ancient Aztec princess. He wishes he knew her - knew the mystery of her story. She can make that saxophone talk; can make it laugh and can make it cry. He decides he is falling in love with her. Ha! Silly old fool!

Finding a ten-pound note, he folds it several times, reducing its bulk. The busker's saxophone case is set on the pavement, inviting passing pedestrians to part with some cash. Joining the latter, trying to be inconspicuous, he adds his folded note to what are mainly one pound and smaller denomination coins already in the case. His contribution is a stupid generosity, an extravagance he can really ill afford. Silly old fool, indeed.

Returning to the bench, he sits down.

The enigmatic busker eventually decides on pastures new. Collecting her takings, she unfolds Willie's banknote and stares at it for some seconds before glancing quickly up. Willie had anticipated an expression of some happy surprise but it is a strangely guarded, suspicious, vaguely anxious expression that rises in her almond shaped eyes as she searches the anonymous mass of passing faces. Casing her saxophone then, she moves quickly on, Willie watching her black-haired head bobbing away with the crowd. Not being that tall, she soon vanishes from view.

And the world continues to wheel by along the pavement, milling around the lure of the shop windows like bluebottles around a rotting carcass.

A well-dressed woman stands on dog's dirt . . . slips . . . half falls . . . steadies . . . glances in disgust at the offending mess, smeared across expensive shoe. Glaring accusingly at the oblivious sea of passing humanity, she hobbles into a shop doorway.

Willie's interest in the activities and foibles of fellow mortals eventually wanes. The day is passing - darkening into late afternoon. Soon, the glow of neon light will thicken along the canyon walls, and the demons and mischief-makers of the night will gather in the back alleys - demons and mischief-makers he remembers well from his younger days - mustering and threatening violence. Back then they couldn't intimidate him. On the contrary, he would seek them out, relishing the confronting of them. But he is growing old now, becoming progressively frailer and afraid - afraid of vague unknown things that are yet to arrive.

What the hell is he doing anyway, sitting on a cold city bench, alone, and two days before Christmas? He pulls the collar of his coat higher around his ears and glances up. The low sky is moving more quickly, much more quickly, than before - unnaturally quickly - the leaden clouds skimming the rooftops at unusual speed. There seems too, to be a sudden rustling scream from the overhead web of twinkling meaningless tinsel that hovers and flaps now like a threatening swarm of alien metallic birds in the darkening city sky. He feels momentarily panicked - faint.

Unaccountably, he thinks of the new woman in the ground floor flat: every day, only one milk bottle - a half pint bottle! He had paid particular attention. Yes, it would appear that she does live alone. And yes, perhaps she too is lonely?

He rises, hunches his shoulders against the icy wind, and heads home.

#

He had hoped that Ewan MacLeod and his wife might have called to bring in the New Year with him. Hogmanay is no time for a man to be alone. A telephone call hadn't been the same as a toast and a shake of the hand. Perhaps it was the prospect of the inevitable whisky had inhibited Ewan. And there was also the shadow of demotion.

Suspension . . . demotion . . . whisky.

Perhaps it had been none of these things. Ewan had his own large family to think about after all.

It was his birthday too. Strange time for a man to be having a birthday. Last day of the year - six minutes before midnight -. just before the bells - like an afterthought - or perhaps a last-minute inconvenience, an irritation? Mind you, not everyone has their birthday heralded by the raising of glasses and the peeling of bells around the entire world!

He smiles faintly and wonders if Sarah and Angus have remembered. He raises his glass to the photographs on the dresser - says 'cheers' for the umpteenth time - and for the umpteenth time the photographs don't acknowledge.

The New Year television programmes have ended, the only sound now being a faint buzzing and with only a white spot visible on a blank screen. 1984 has come and gone - Orwell's year! The man had guessed it right. It had become a world of Big Brothers, of emergent machines called personal computers. The individual had become but a number, his individual importance diminished, his existence being increasingly meddled with by men of privilege and power but, in human terms, of no consequence.

He decides that the Hogmanay programmes had been a parade of over-sentimental rubbish: Lowland men, and even English men, dressed in kilts, emulating the Highland men they had historically despised - had help destroy.

The comedian, Rikkie Fulton, had been good though. He had laughed out loud. He liked Rikkie Fulton.

#

It is New Year's day and he is glad to be on duty, glad of the distraction.

Ibrox football stadium is a seething sea of two colours - blue, and green and white. Protestant and Catholic. Rangers and Celtic.

Football is what they call it, a game, but they are wrong. It is more serious than that. It is a matter of life and death - a primeval tribal thing . . . war . . . uncompromising religious hatred and bigotry, a terrible frightening animal thing. You can see it in the wash of pale tense faces, hear it in the baying snarl of the wolf crowd.

The result is a draw - one goal each. That is good because nobody has won and that avoids inane triumphalism - lessens the likelihood of trouble, lessens but doesn't altogether preclude. A scuffle breaks out behind the grandstand, a blue scarf knocking a green and white scarf to the ground and unleashing vicious mindless kicks. More blue and more green and white scarves close in. Uniformed police, drawing batons, converge along with plain clothes men on the wheeling pack.

A low growl emanates from deep in Alex Craig's throat as he rushes forward and grabs a random green and white scarf from the periphery of the melee; a youth of about fifteen, pimple faced but boyishly handsome, blond hair, blue eyes - the universal blue eyed inoffensive kid from next door. The blue eyes widen in alarm.

A Black Maria reverses through the metal stadium gates, dark and ominous and sporting small barred windows. The police driver leaps out and throws open the rear doors. Alex Craig's knuckles whiten on the tightening green and white scarf. Veins bulge on the youth's reddening face. He tries to speak, to protest. The sound is a restricted croak. Alex Craig hoists him into the rear of the Black Maria and sends him sprawling with an unnecessary rough shove. The alarm on the youth's face turns to outrage and indignation.

'Hey, officer! Ah didnie dae onythin! Ah wus ony watchin' tha . . . '

Alex Craig moves forward and punches him hard in the base of the stomach and he falls to his knees, gasping. More scarves are being bundled into the Maria and Alex Craig jumps down.

Willie's face is ashen. 'For God's sake, Craig! I saw that! You aren't judge and jury! Do that again and I'll personally break your arm!'

Alex Craig is breathing hard with emotion, his lips clamped tight across his teeth in a mirthless dog grin.

'Fuck off! Teuchter!'

Somebody grabs Willie's shoulder. It is inspector MacLeod beckoning him aside.

'There's been another one, Willie. Another killing.'

'Jesus! Same fellow?'

'No doubts about it. Yet another riddle. But a subtle difference this time. Instead of the usual *more to come* it is now *almost done*. Hopefully, this signals an end to the madness.'

'Glasgow?'

'No, goddammit, he is back on Skye.'

#

The emergency meeting at police H.Q has been droning on for almost an hour, the Chief Inspector himself and most of the Big Brass from C.I.D being present.

Although the central heating is set full blast and the atmosphere is oppressive with cigarette and pipe smoke, Willie is running a cold sweat. He hasn't been feeling too well, on and off, for several weeks. It is as if some beast has entered him and is persistently gnawing at his innards. His thoughts have drifted beyond the briefing room windows when he realises he is being personally addressed by the Chief Inspector.

' . . . so, it has been agreed Morrison. You are the obvious choice: a Skye man with long experience of police work in Glasgow. Ties you in with both of the murder locations. You are fluent in the Gaelic language, and in view of the Skye connection, we have to consider the possibility of the killer being a Gael. We want yourself and detective constable Alex Craig to team up with the Skye force for a few days, compare notes, get your heads together and see what you can come up with.'

Due to a family bereavement, Alex Craig isn't present.

'I don't think I will need have constable Craig along sir.'

'Oh? And why not?'

'I have my reasons sir . . . personal reasons.'

Caught by surprise, he has reacted to the Alex Craig suggestion on the spur of the moment and immediately regrets the 'personal' reference. Finding himself in a corner now, he will require to explain himself, while not wishing to cause Alex Craig any harm.

'Goddammit Morrison, you are a member of the police force. There are no such obstacles as personal reasons to police work. And what might these reasons be, may I ask? Remember that we are all senior staff here today. Anything that is said here won't go beyond these four walls.'

Willie remains silent a moment, gauging his answer, struggling to avoid using the term *prejudices*. 'Alex Craig, in my opinion, has certain . . . eh . . . set opinions which could possibly flavour his better judgement in certain situations, situations such as the investigation presently under discussion. Speaking strictly as a police officer, and in the best interests of this particular investigation, I judge that to be reason enough.'

'Set opinions? What do you mean by that, Morrison?'

'It is only my judgement, perhaps only my instinct. To elaborate and perhaps sow incorrect seeds would be unfair.'

The Chief Inspector glances at the assembly before him and snaps his folder shut.

'You are an old timer Morrison. You know the game, know it as well as any man on the force. And I know you as a fair and decent man. I will accept your judgement for these reasons. But I will remind you, and all of us here, that the police force is a team and no single man is bigger than that team. Also, we have strict vetting of recruits. Detective Constable Craig was subject to that vetting and passed with flying colours.'

'I know that sir, and my judgement is made only in its application to this particular investigation. I said it was only an instinct, a gut feeling. I could be wrong. I am fully aware that constable Craig is an enthusiastic and dedicated officer, it's just that I think that in this particular investigation, we would only, eh . . . distract one another.'

The Chief Inspector sighs. Behind him, a yellow faced clock is talking to itself on the wall. Somebody shuffles his feet. Somebody else coughs. The Chief Inspector continues: 'Well gentlemen, I think that that covers it for the time being. Thank you for your close attention. Morrison, would you remain behind please. You too, Inspector MacLeod, if you don't mind.'

The Big Brass rise to their feet and scrape en masse across the wooden floor towards the door. Ewan MacLeod glances sidelong at Willie - the despairing glance of a concerned friend. Seated on a wooden chair with his shoulders hunched, Willie doesn't look at all well. A vacant film has veiled the natural warmth of his eyes, the spray of wrinkles at their corners showing up as being deep notched. Silver is sprouting from the temples of his thick black hair. Ewan anguishes at how quickly he seems to be ageing of late.

The Chief Inspector has risen from behind his desk and moved to the window. Silently surveying the city, as if for evidence of pillage and rape, he is wearing his severe Chief Inspector expression. The severe expression doesn't last, however, quickly becoming an endearingly cute expression, this being on account of the fact that Glasgow would, inexplicably, appear to be behaving herself, and the Chief Inspector is very grateful and pleased about that - very suspicious, but very pleased. When he speaks, it is in the Gaelic language.

*(Not another Gaelic man! Just as well Alex Craig isn't present – he would be spitting nails! THREE Gaelic men – teuchters – running the show! All in together, boys!)*

'*No mean city* is what they are calling her,' says the Chief Inspector, '*No mean city*. And no place for a Highland man to spend his life, say I - no place at all. So why do we keep on coming, generation after generation of us? Can you answer me that one, Willie?

The talking wall clock claims the silence again, Willie vacantly staring at it, not seeing it, taking his time in replying.

'Because we have no choice, I suppose. Because we have to live. Because we did nothing about it.'

Double checking that Glasgow isn't pulling the wool over his eyes and taking him for a mug, the Chief Inspector relaxes and leans his hands on the window jambs.

'*It,* Willie? Did nothing about, *it*? What is it you'll be meaning now by *it*?'

'Exploitation? Governmental unconcern? Historical neglect? The invasion by strangers? Perhaps I don't even know.'

'The invasion by strangers?' repeats the Chief Inspector ruefully.

'Ach well,' Ewan MacLeod buts in, 'at least we still have the old tongue. And our sweet memories - memories of old Gaeldom - of home, of the old people and the old ways, albeit from afar now, unfortunately.'

'And maybe that is the only way we can now tolerate it Ewan - from afar', says Willie. 'Because we know that we won't, ever again, find it as our memory will always cling to it - unchanged! But it has inevitably changed, of course, as we ourselves have changed. Gaeldom, as we knew and loved it, only remains now in the mothballs of memory. Och no, the Gaelic times have run their course. And what can you do about it? Time marches on. And then again, if it comes to the bit, does it really matter?'

The three men fall silent. Ewan MacLeod utters a silly little chortle, not from any sense of amusement - a meaningless yet somehow necessary little sound, necessary in that it serves to give reply to unanswerable questions, serves to smother the endless counting-down of the clock and the dusty rustle of Gaelic men's fading lives.

Iain Ferguson

*Oh, Skye,*
*It was springtime when I left you,*
*so very long ago.*
*And the young grass was thrusting*
*through the last of winter's snow.*
*But when I returned 'twas autumn,*
*blowing dead leaves all around.*
*And another race of people*
*trod on mine beneath the ground*

# FOUR

The carriage heating is non-existent, and that is a diabolical outrage; the drawn expressions of the white-faced sprinkle of passengers can testify to that. The coldest night so far of this coldest of winters - and the bloody heating doesn't work! Yes, a diabolical outrage! And all these inexplicable stops and starts! A sign of the times, of course, and an indication of how far British Railways has deteriorated since its glory days.

But, then again, it is the West Highland Line after all, the poor relation, so perhaps it is no surprise.

Sitting alone, Willie pulls the collar of his coat higher around his ears, hunches his shoulders and sips at his whisky.

The carriage is a central corridor affair, with seats and tables running along both sides - a yawing clanking tube, illuminated by dismal yellow lights. Sipping more whisky, he scrapes the ice from the window and peers into the night. The train is moving at an infuriating crawl, the square window reflections rising and falling, sliding and distorting, on the banked snow by the side of the track.

The landscape of earlier has changed, the hills now mountains, higher and fiercer, the glint of a full frosty moon sparkling on their jagged snow-capped crests. The train has crept into the Highlands proper, is now approaching the small isolated settlement that is Bridge of Orchy. He has travelled the West Highland Line often, knows it like the back of his hand, although the last time has been ten years past…ten years since he has last seen the land of his childhood. A mixture of nostalgic excitement and inexplicable anxiety grips him.

He glances at the two women sat opposite, across the central corridor. The younger one is doggedly persevering with her novel while the tweedy matron, across the table from her, is irritably spinning an empty gin glass and glaring over a mountain of Angora scarf at the novel's cover, not really seeing it in her general discomfort and disgust. The immaculate set of her ostentatious and rather ridiculous hair-do seems a shade less perky than it was on leaving Glasgow - an outrageous three hours before.

The hair-do has Willie mesmerised. A mass of hair coils intertwined and piled high, it lies plonked on the crown of the matron's head in the form of a beehive. The last time he can recall seeing its like, was in old paintings from the Versailles Palace of Louis X1V.

Positioned as the beehive is, Willie is puzzled as to how, in apparent defiance of gravity, it remains in place. In consideration for the matron's dignity, he is very concerned about possible slippage, and also, if he is reading the lady correctly, she is no stranger to screaming hysterics. He pessimistically sets the life expectancy of the ridiculous creation at a further forty-five minutes - max! In addition to mesmerising him, therefore, the hair-do is also setting him very much on edge.

The matron rises suddenly, the gin glass still in her hand, and half stomps half staggers down a by now well-worn path towards the buffet bar, Willie contemplating the indignant gyrations of her ample buttocks with some detached amusement. A sense of surrealism has been added by the munch-mallow, on which she has unknowingly sat, and which now clings, smeared across the expensive tweed of her skirt - a derisive pink smudge. Avoiding eye contact with the Louis X1V beehive, Willie smiles to himself.

Eventually, the matron returns with glass fully replenished and pitches back into her seat, and Willie scratches at the reformed ice on the carriage window and peers out. And time and the train grind on.

After a while, Willie too finds himself contemplating an empty glass but he has predetermined to temper his consumption - to pace himself. He suffers twenty more minutes of this unfamiliar 'tempering' thing before he begins to weaken, and a further twenty seconds before he breaks.

Och, to hell! It is cold beyond human sufferance. A man needs heat, goddammit! He glances at the matron. Her glass is again empty, her disgusted expression meantime, having eased to a rosy flush of apathetic surrender to fate.

Willie rises to his feet.

'Excuse me madam, may I fill you up?'

The glaze of the matron's eyes swings towards him, a slow jerky sweep, over-lined by a frown.

'I beg your pardon?!'

'Your glass, madam. May I fill you up?'

Understanding registers. 'Oh! . . . why…that's, that's very sweet of you sir. Well…yes….yes, why not? I wouldn't normally but the cold is intolerable. Just a SMALL one now! Thank you so very much.' She flutters her eyelashes, affecting an absurd maiden coyness. Too late, Willie realises that she has exceeded her limit, has already had several too many.

'And you, miss?'

The younger woman glances up from her novel and smiles. 'No thank you. I'm fine, just fine. Thank you very much.' From her accent, the younger woman is obviously Highland.

Twenty minutes later, accompanied by jolts, hissings and the rattle of metal couplings, the train grinds to yet another unscheduled series of stops and starts, the fifth since leaving Glasgow.

'Oh Lord! Not again!' laments the matron.

The window has once more iced over, and once more Willie scrapes it clear. They have stopped on Rannoch Moor, about the most desolate and savage expanses of emptiness in Western Europe, silvered now by moon and snow - a seemingly endless ancient wilderness.

As he gazes out, Willie finds himself wondering why it was, over the last decade or so, that he had so resisted a persistent urge to return to these silent places of his ancestors and his roots. In attempted explanation, he had once reminded Ewan that for centuries strangers had viewed these northern lands and their people as a challenge, a challenge to be overcome - a resource to be exploited. And as these strangers had panted in ever increasing numbers northward, with a covetous glint in the eye and a breathless determination on change, his own people, the Gaelic people, had shrunk as a result, while yet few, far too few of these same strangers had cared a damn, or had bothered to see the remnants for what they were - a priceless cultural treasure. And wasn't it because of that, surely, that he and his kind - exiles - had shied away, had confined the Gaelic homelands to memory?

All these tumbling thoughts! He realises that the whisky is going to his head.

Breathing hard, he presses his face against the cold of the glass and continues to gaze at the silvered crests of the distant mountains. Sensing the heave and beckon of subterranean roots sighing towards him from the North West, he feels awed by the beauty of the moment. If only it could remain forever like that, a poignant and beautiful moment. Ah, but then there is *Time* - the ancient enemy - *Time!* And *Time*, of course, will destroy it. Because of *Time*, all, absolutely everything that he cherishes and loves, must one day vanish - a terrible inevitability.

'*Time, the endless idiot, runs screaming round the world*'

He had thought it and said it on impulse. Realising he had said it aloud, he glances awkwardly at the two women opposite, who are staring curiously back.

The flush of the matron's face is, by now, a crimson rage of abandon - the chill of the carriage has magically vanished, as has stupid propriety, and even more stupid inhibition. Yes, by now she is being devoured by the flames of wild abandon - and enjoying every delicious liberating minute of it! Euphoria and sensuous desires, too long denied by widowhood and by 'appearances', are reasserting themselves, desires honed carnal and keen now by an excess of gin, hormonal rhythms and a persistent massaging of the nether regions by the unending rock and sway of a British Railways carriage.

Willie glances compulsively at the Louis X1V beehive, horrified by its sudden change of position. Those prone to frivolity would no doubt regard the new position as a 'jaunty angle', but to Willie the angle spells imminent catastrophe. Not only that, one of the individual hair-coils is showing early signs of uncoiling.

*Slippage! . . . Uncoiling!*

The nightmare he dreaded has begun!

Not wanting to be around when female hysterics kick off, he decides to close his eyes and count sheep.

The matron, meantime, is gazing, cow eyed, at this man in such close proximity opposite her; so charming, so sensitive - so obviously alone;

a gentleman who had bought a lady a drink. Two drinks, in actual fact - two large very generous drinks!; a gallant gentleman - such a very rare breed these days! A prince charming upon a white horse.

'Why, sshir,' she twitters, slurring her words at the same time, 'that wash byoofitable . . . wash byoofitabubble and rather . . . rather . . . profound! Wild and byoofitabubble . . . and . . . and . . . yesh - LONELY!'

Feeling obliged to cease the sheep-count, Willie opens his eyes.

'It's the whisky, madam. Just too much whisky, nothing more.' He smiles weakly and lifts his empty glass in awkward salute. Well, well, talking to himself now? A sure sign of advanced alcoholism - or madness!

The train approaches Fort William, the matron's destination, two and a half hours late. Staggering to her feet, she reaches for her suitcase on the overhead rack and totters backwards as the carriage jerkily rounds a curve of the track, landing her in a half giggling, half screeching heap on Willie's lap.

'Oh! DO pardon me sshir. Ha! Ha! Ha! Do pardon me! I trust I didn't hurt shoo?'

'No damage done at all, madam. Think nothing of it.'

'But my weight, shir! Ha! Ha! Ha! Far too mush over-weight shoo know?'

'Not at all, madam. Just ripeness. Ripe womanly prime.'

The matron glances at him quickly, further abandon, further carnality in her eyes. The rogue hair-coil has completely uncoiled by now and is waggling about.

'Ha! Ha! Ha! You're sho gallant shir. What little white liesh! What a naughty naughty boy shoo are. Ha! Ha! Ha!' she twitters, struggling to her feet. Willie clutches at the middle-aged blubber of her waist in assistance, a large portion of munch-mallow, meantime, having transferred its allegiance from tweed skirt to the knee of his trousers.

'I'll help you down with your suitcase madam.'

'Shoo might be shtopping off at Fort William shoorself, sshirr?'

(What WAS she saying!)The matron realises, too late, the veiled invitation in her own impulsive question. If her face wasn't already as flushed as it could possibly be, and if she wasn't consumed by euphoria and abandon, she would have flushed.

'I'm afraid not madam, it's Mallaig I'm headed for.'

'Ha! Ha! Ha!' The Matron's laughter is confused, absurdly little girlish.

'Well sshir, it's been real shweet meeting shoo. And thank shoo for the drinkie poos, although I mush shay that shoo hash made me rather tippshy - shoo naughty naughty boy! My shister is picking me up at the station. What WILL she say? Very relishus you know! Violently teetotal! Ha! Ha! Ha! '

'Oh, I'm sure your sister will understand, Madam. When she learns of the cold and delays you have endured.'

'Ha! Ha! Ha!. Won't shpeak to me for daysh! It'll be cold compresshes to fevered brow, and retreats to darkened roomsh - shilly bitch! Ha! Ha! Ha!'

The matron turns to the younger woman. 'Goodbye miss.'

Willie hands her her suitcase.

'Well, goodbye sshir. Ha! Ha! Ha!'

'Goodbye madam. Take care.'

'Perhaps I hash no opshun! Ha! Ha! Ha! . . . ' (Oops-a-daisy! There she was - at it again! What WAS she saying!) '...Ha! Ha! Ha! . . . but I shertainly will. And shoo too. Goodbye! Goodbye!'

She lurches down the carriage corridor, the weight of the suitcase held before her forcing her into a mincing, waddling half run, while Willie, rather guiltily, decides that she reminds him at that moment of a tweed bedecked version of Two Ton Tessie O'Shea.

The train grinds to a sudden halt and 'Tessie O'Shea' catapults, a screeching giggling heap, into the knot of already traumatised passengers impatiently gathered at the carriage door, the Louis X1V beehive meantime having totally succumbed to the brutal assaults of drunken human motion.

# LIFT ME, DADDY

Slippage and uncoiling have won over the day!

Fort William train station being a dead end, means that what had been the front of the train going in is the rear of the train going out again and requiring that it retrace its steps for approximately a mile, until the fork in the rails - one fork heading south to Glasgow, the other heading north west to Mallaig. The dead end also requires that the engine be uncoupled and repositioned at the 'new' front end, or replaced by a fresh stand-by engine, a procedure that further requires the train to remain stationary for approximately a quarter of an hour.

Scowling at that prospect now, Willie sinks deeper into his seat as the carriage brakes are de-iced, the buffet bar re-stocked and hasty repairs are made to the heating system. In the meantime, carriage doors bang and porters' trolleys squeak - and the new engine groans in anticipation of the iron hardship of the black mountainous journey ahead.

Willie and the young woman are the only remaining passengers in their particular carriage. Repairs to the heating problems are quickly proving to have been a dismal failure. In actual fact, talks of repairs are a gross exaggeration - a 'white lie', put about by the on-duty junior heating engineer responsible for the task. His heart isn't in it. Most of the problem emanates from externally located pipe-work. His fingers are frost-bitten and useless, and it's two and a half hours beyond his usual clock-off time. Sod it! Frozen to the bone, he is desperate to get home to the fire, devour his re-heated dinner, stroke the cat and tickle his wife.

Eventually, the train grinds westwards, towards Mallaig and the evening steamer to Skye. The air temperature, incredibly, is still dropping and Willie, armed with a fresh half bottle of whisky, is becoming more intoxicated and increasingly morbid. The young woman has abandoned her novel and is miserably hunched in the depths of her coat collars. It has to be well below freezing.

She becomes aware of Willie surveying her and she glances across and smiles - a broad warm smile.

'You'll be having the Gaelic miss, I'm thinking?' he says.

'As well as you'll be having her yourself, I'm sure,' is her Gaelic reply.

'Och aye. I just thought so now. Have you ever experienced such cold, miss? You'll be having a wee dram to be warming you up?'

'No. Honestly. Thank you all the same.' She smiles again and retreats deeper into her coat collars. In the ensuing silence Willie scrapes the ice from the window for the umpteenth time. A bank of cloud has smothered the moon and beyond the rise and fall of the window reflections inky darkness stretches to eternity. Teuchter land - land of the Gaels! What would Alex Craig have made of it, had he been here?

*Every man has his prejudices*

Yes, Alex Craig had been right in that but, goddammit, what are Willie's own - what the hell are his own? He gulps more whisky. Ah! Deliciously warming, gently befuddling, honing the sharp edges off grey reality.

And the train grinds on…and on…and on…into what seems to have become an endless and surreal journey into darkness.

*'In the middle of the journey of my life I came to myself in a dark wood where the straight way was lost.'*

He had spoken absently - again aloud - to the passing night beyond the window.

The young woman studies him for some minutes before she speaks.

'So, you are fond of the quotations then?'

She has decided that there is something infinitely lonely about this man, this stranger, who is talking to himself. Normally, such behaviour might have put her on her guard, but instead she is finding herself warming to him, becoming increasingly aware of some complex sadness. There is, too, something indefinably 'nice' about him, something 'nice' in his face. It's the eyes mostly, in their nest of wrinkles, and she is sensing that not that far beyond their sadness, is laughter also, a sense of fun and compassion. And are the eyes not the windows on the soul?

The young woman's question registers and his eyes slide round upon her smile, clinging gladly to its warmth. In his inebriation, he is beyond his earlier embarrassment. But - talking to himself, spouting quotations aloud to himself! Yes, he must truly be losing control of his senses.

'What was that earlier one, that earlier quotation? *Time, the endless idiot...?*' continues the young woman.

'*....runs screaming around the world,* miss'

'Yes, that's it. The lady that was here certainly seemed to like it. I must say, I like it too. Your own?'

The question amuses him and he smiles faintly. 'Och no miss, I don't, unfortunately, have such power of the words. It's only other greater men's words I spout. Only other men's words. It was Carson McCullers said it miss.'

'Can't say I have heard of him.'

'He was a she, miss.'

His eyes slide back to the whisky bottle. The young woman sees fresh desolation flicker across their grey sadness and she is consumed by a wave of compassion and, unaccountably, sudden affection. Confined to a freezing rattling yellow-lit tube, yawing westwards on a black winter's night, she has found herself alone with a total stranger, an intoxicated rambling stranger, as her sole companion. She should be experiencing alarm perhaps, but isn't. And it isn't just the reassuring bond of common language, common culture, that is making her unafraid, but the dawning realisation that here might be that increasingly rarest of creatures - a genuinely nice, genuinely gentle human being.

'You know, I might just have that wee dram after all.'

The young woman's words ease into the emptiness of his thoughts like a warm breeze and his face brightens.

'Och, of course! Of course!'

'Mind if I slide across?'

He staggers to his feet and removes his hold-all from the seat opposite. 'Of course! Of course!' He pours two whiskies. The young woman raises hers towards him:

'Slainte!'

'Ach miss, slainte indeed. Slainte! Slainte!'

'How nice it is to be speaking the Gaelic again. The entire journey from Glasgow it looked as if we were the only Gaelic speakers in the carriage. Did you notice that?'

'Och miss, how could I avoid noticing it? The Mallaig train - the train to the Highlands and Hebrides - and carrying mainly strangers. How times are changing, and how terribly quickly at that. I can remember, not so very long ago, when it was the Gaels outdid the non-Gaels on the Mallaig train. Perhaps that only happens now when she is travelling south - travelling in the *emptying* direction.'

He is gazing at the young woman with a sad, cow eyed and decidedly inebriated expression which she finds endearingly pathetic, and her smile widens.

'You don't need words of your own, you know. Even if they are other men's words, if you can appreciate them, it means they are in you too; have been in you all along, just waiting to be triggered into motion. What was it again that the lady said about the earlier quotation? *Wild and lonely?* I am Cathy, by the way. Cathy McKinnon' She holds out her hand and Willie grasps it firmly, feeling the soft creamy warmth that has defied the cold of the carriage.

'Willie Morrison, Cathy. It's certainly a great pleasure to be meeting you, to be sure.'

With his smile, the nest of wrinkles deepens around his eyes. He notices that Cathy's left hand carries neither wedding nor engagement ring. Annoyed with himself for consciously noticing that, he lets her right-hand slip away. He gazes into her smiling face, fresh and young and trusting, while he himself is old enough to be her father.

'Is that how you feel, Willie?' Cathy raises her whisky to her lips.

'Pardon?'

'Wild and lonely! Is that how you feel?'

'Oh . . . wild? Once, when I was young, I suppose you might have called me wild. Wildness isn't such a terrible thing in the young, provided there is no malice or violence in it. A certain wildness is to be expected, perhaps hoped for in the young. But I am older now and such things as wildness should have long left me. Wildness in an old man, Cathy, is only foolishness.'

'Oh, come on Willie. Mid to late-fifties is what I would guess. That's not old. Life is only beginning.' She sips at her whisky and Willie pours himself another.

'That leaves *lonely* Willie. Do you feel *lonely*?'

He lowers his gaze and toys with his glass. 'And you are a schoolteacher, Cathy. That's what I would guess.'

'Correct guess, Willie. I'm impressed. And you?'

He hesitates. 'A policeman.'

Cathy raises her eyebrows. 'Well well, a policeman? You could have fooled me. You don't look at all like a policeman, I must say.'

'And how is a policeman supposed to look, Cathy?'

'Assessing. Not believing what you say. Suspicious. Always at his work. Difficult to trust.'

'That covers a fair bit of ground. Not very flattering ground. I look like that?'

Cathy brushes his hand briefly. 'No, Willie. You don't. Not in the very least.'

And the train groans on, westward and slightly northward, winding along the frozen feet of the black iron mountains towards the fishing village that is Mallaig.

The station platform is filmed by slushy snow when they eventually arrive. Willie lifts Cathy's luggage onto a porter's barrow and they walk towards the small knot of people waiting by the barrier at the platform end.

'You said you were headed for the Skye steamer yourself, Cathy?'

'Yes Willie, I am.' She catches his arm suddenly. She is smiling again, her eyes and teeth sparkling in the reflection of the dim platform lights.

'Colin, my boyfriend, is waiting Willie. Thanks for your company.

And for the wee dram.'

- *Ah yes! Of course! Young love! Young love likes to be alone.-*

There is genuine warmth, but also a sudden earnest pity in her smile, the latter putting a chill in Willie's heart. 'And Willie, there's no need to feel lonely. Please don't feel alone. We will bump into each other again sometime. Good luck!' She kisses him briefly on the cheek, smiles some more and moves towards the grinning young man at the barrier.

'Goodbye Cathy, goodbye.' He says it softly, to himself, the whining night wind whipping the words, as they are uttered, to oblivion.

'Goodbye, Cathy.'

Realising that he is touching the kiss on his cheek, he abruptly drops his hand and staggers forward.

Stupid old man! Yes! Stupid, stupid old man!

He catches up with the porter who says in Gaelic that it's wild weather. He agrees with the man: it is very wild weather indeed. And he feels the beast that has entered him stir and gnaw. He still isn't feeling too well.

The steamer is rolling and pitching at the far end of the quay, one of several berthed vessels, some sending beams of lonely light starring across the sleety surfaces. Apart from a few fleeing human voices in the wind, the only sound is the slap of wave on metal hull and, somewhere, the deep throated throb of idling engines, the characteristic bustle and seagull screech of daytime Mallaig being noticeably absent. Only a lone maverick gull still forages for fish scraps on the quay, his companions already a necklace of roosting white blotches on riggings, masts and harbour rooftops.

Above the wind, the full frosty moon has shaken off the snow clouds and is silvering the anger of the sea and surrounding mountain ranges. On the horizon, across the Sound of Sleat, Skye is a black silent mass, a prehistoric sleeping thing, her dog-tooth silhouette edged by a faint blue sparkle of ice.

Across that strip of sea lies the island of his early childhood - of his roots and the very core of his soul; a land of blasted heath, black volcanic rock, mountain, heather, moorland and peat bog - a land of smoky memories, evoking free-roaming childhood, and laughter, and joy.

Ah, but yet also, in parallel, are memories of death and sorrow, sometime poverty, grim religious restraint and rebuke; memories enshrouded in days of seemingly endless sunshine, while yet also days of seemingly endless wind and rain. Across that narrow strip of sea, lies a minute fragment of the great planet Earth, but a fragment world renowned for its misty mystique and savage Celtic beauty - *Eilean a cheo (Isle of Mist)* - Isle of Skye!

As he looks, his thoughts jell, as they invariably do in relation to Skye, in a total confusion of emotions. So many times, in his city exile, he has contemplated these confusions, striving to pinpoint their reasons, their root reasons, because there is more to these confusions than the mere invasion by strangers. Oh yes, it is much more complex than that, and on so many occasions he had almost got it, the answer, tantalisingly hovering on the very edge of understanding, only for it to drift away as he had breathlessly reached out to grasp it.

#

His stay on Skye will last just under two weeks. The island roads had remained relatively clear of snow but the bus to the north of the island, on that morning following the train journey, had still arrived at the glen crossroads some twenty minutes behind schedule.

His uncle Finlay isn't at the crossroads to meet him. But that's Finlay, one of a vanishing Gaelic bachelor breed; used to living alone, happy to be living alone, unmarried: - *'Och, women can't help but be getting in the way'* - a breed unconcerned by clocks and public transport schedules, motivated only by the cycle of crops and the schedules of tending and feeding animals, guided only by the mood and drifting progress of individual days. Yes, Finlay has animals to attend to, and anyway, what is the good of fuss? It isn't that Finlay isn't warmly expectant of Willie's visit. He likes Willie. In fact, he might even admit to his expectancy stretching to a fair degree of silent excitement.

They bump into one another on the old dirt road, by the gable of the byre. Finlay is clutching a bale of hay to his chest and looks taken mildly by surprise.

'Och, well, well Willie, it's yourself, eh? Well, well, eh?' He wipes his right hand on his dungarees and offers it in welcome. 'Och, well well Willie. Och man, it's grand you're looking, just grand, eh?' His Gaelic conversation is liberally punctuated by characteristic nervous chuckles, every other sentence being a question, invariably rhetorical, the last one being a shocked and deliberate lie; Willie is looking far from 'grand', his face being ashen and gaunt and drenched in sweat.

'Och well yourself Finlay, and it's grand yourself is looking too.' That is no lie. Finlay is the picture of ruddy rural health, the clasp of his swollen sausage fingers being bands of crushing iron around Willie's soft city hands.

A moistness has appeared in Finlay's light blue eyes, reminding Willie anew of his uncle's strange weakness: some sentimental softness that threatens but never actually achieves emotional breakdown when he is confronted by someone or something linking him to his childhood or to the Gaelic past.

'Och Willie, I should have met you at the crossroads, eh? But with the cows bawling for their hay I clean forgot the time.' He casts the bale to the side of the road. 'But they can we waiting for it; will do them no harm, eh? Give me that hold-all man. Och, well well Willie, eh?'

Approaching the old family house, Willie can smell the burning peat - the ancient and evocative smell of burning peat - hanging in the frosty air; and that is to set the scene for a week and a bit of nostalgic memories of childhood, and its smells, and sounds and sights.

Settled in the house, they have a few mandatory drams and, since Willie isn't really that hungry, a buttered scone. As Finlay later attends to the animals, an exhausted Willie falls asleep in his chair beside a roaring peat fire, awaking only in time to help his uncle set the table for dinner - a dinner of traditional salted herring and potatoes.

'Well Finlay, it's a long time since I've tasted a good salted herring and potatoes; and washed down with milk fresh from the cow.'

'Och, nothing to beat it Willie, eh? The Highlanders of the old days were brought up on salted herring and potatoes. And no harm it did them either, eh? No harm at all. Big strong bonnie men it produced. Not many of them left nowadays though, eh?'

'Aye. Two world wars had a lot to answer for there Finlay. Sent them home in boxes they did, thousands upon thousands of them - those of them they could find enough bits of!'

'And a fine lot of good it did the Highlands, a fine lot they cared about us when the whole mess was done, eh? *Remembered in war, forgotten in peace.* Politicians and their promises! Just broken promises, eh? Rogues and liars, just rogues and liars, the whole bunch of them! But what's the use in talking, eh?'

'Aye, Finlay, what's the use in talking, right enough'

There is a short silence.

'Talking about the old days, the place isn't quite the same with the electric light. You miss the oil and Tilley lamps. They gave a softer, more homely atmosphere, with their flickering flames casting shadows to jumping in the corners; yes, those old lamps gave a cosyness, an intimacy.'

Distant memories are flooding over Willie, and he pours himself and Finlay another dram.

'Remember when we were young Finlay, and the whole family together; the long winter nights huddled around the peat fire, passing the time with *ceilidhs* and ghost stories and all the while the wind howling? Aye, the shifting shadows in the corners fair frightened us back then. Ah yes, and I can still picture the *bodach* and the *cailleach* - shennair and granny - in the room here yet, basking in the glow from family closeness. Bless their dear souls.'

'Och, they did us proud, eh? And times were hard too. But man, they were better times for all that. Harder but better, eh? You talk about *ceilidhs* and ghost stories. Well Willie, that's all long gone; just damned television now. A man can't be finding time to be giving you a kind look nowadays, or to be even talking to you, for gawking at the damned television. People just don't visit like they used to. The young don't come *ceilidhing* with the pipes accordions and the fiddles anymore - if there were any young folk left, that is, eh?'

Finlay pauses to fill his pipe.

'All these incomers has a lot to do with things too. White Settlers on the island everywhere you look. Remember Glenvale, eh? Nothing but White Settlers. You will be hard pushed to find a Gaelic family left in Glenvale nowadays Willie, eh? And the Glenvale situation is quickly spreading to all corners of the island - if not the entire Highlands! Even up the glen here! Old Norman McSween died two years ago and it's a retired southern couple has his house now. Even up the glen, eh? No place is sacred. Nice enough people on the whole, but their ways is so different - always after changing things. Gaeldom was long a place of spirituality – a connection with ancestral land, but the spirituality has been broken. The harmony has been broken. The old community spirit is gone.'

There is another brief silence

'Worst of all though, it is the White Settler is forcing the house prices on the island sky high; so high that the locals can't compete, and our young, our future life's blood, are forced to leave. Och man, it's the White Settler is putting the final nail in the Gaelic coffin, eh? Just killing us and the old ways off they are, just killing us off! But what's the use in talking, eh?'

Finlay's pipe has gone out and he relights it.

Willie surveys him silently a moment. 'Are things really as bad as that, as bad as people are saying?'

'Dammit man, you can't move for them keeping an eye on you. Anonymous calls to the police if a crofter shoots a bird or a beast that threatens his sheep. Conservation is what they call it, eh? Many of them are retired folks with time to kill, and with plenty money. Others are city folk, with sentimental impractical ideas - looking for causes - folk who know nothing about the land and its ways. Och aye, conservation is all very fine, but it is our living, our survival, is at stake. You can't even be reclaiming bogland nowadays but there is some White Settler demanding an enquiry into the effects on the wildlife - and to hell with the crofter meantime! Conservationists! Save the whale and to hell with the Gael!'

Finlay spits his disgust into the fire.

Getting a strong voice in local politics too. Now, that's when they really have us finished, eh? White Settler Tory councillors! It will be the White Settler interest - conservation - will take precedence over our interests, our desire to continue our traditional livelihood and way of life. Och aye, and it's all well entrenched already!'

Again, Finlay spits into the fire, momentarily mesmerised by the spittle sizzling on a hot peat. 'And just as bad is all them picnics that is moving in. Och, but what's the use in talking, eh?'

'Picnics? How do you mean picnics, Finlay?'

'Och, you know; with long hair and dirt, and doing no work; just doing no work at all - except the social security! You know, eh? Picnics!'

Willie collapses back in his chair with laughter.

'Beatniks! Beatniks Finlay! Och, man alive - picnics! Man, man, you're too much - picnics!' His laughter eventually subsides to periodic sobs of hilarity. 'Oh Finlay, I can't remember when I laughed so much - picnics!' And he is off again.

Composure reasserting itself, the episode eases the conversation towards a more light-hearted vein. And the two men drink and reminisce and laugh into the wee small hours of the morning; until the peat fire has burned itself out, cinders settling and grey ash sifting through the bars of the grate: until further conversation is an unnecessary intrusion upon the intimacy of memory and individual thoughts; thoughts stirring to the backdrop of a moaning wind, prowling the empty blackness of the winter glen outside.

Eventually, time arrives for sleep, for sleep and the shadowed company of dreams - or nightmares, perhaps.

Iain Ferguson

# **FIVE**

Willie isn't sure what has wakened him the following morning; perhaps Finlay rising in the room next door, but it is early - predawn, which means that neither of them have had much sleep.

He finds himself in the attic bedroom he remembers so well, with its sloping ceiling and the skylight window directly over the bed. He had shared a bed in this very room as a youngster with two brothers; the older and more restless Roddy, who would eventually emigrate to America, and the younger, artistic Donnie - now dead.

The memory of it comes to him afresh now in engulfing waves of half sleep, half dream, surging and ebbing, persistent pulse beats tattooing attention in the back of his mind to cold wild nights from Hebridean winters long past; primeval savage nights, when this small attic room had donned the mantle of lair, of den: nights when the iced Atlantic winds hoisted their skirts and rampaged landward, screeching down the glen and howling around the gables, a demented banshee, shaking the house to its very foundations until it seemed it must surely crash to the ground. At such times the young brothers - himself, Roddy and Donnie - would peer anxiously from the blanket depths, wide-eyed fox cubs pressing close, seeking the reassuring touch and scent of siblings.

His thoughts remain fixed on the memory.

Ah yes, Roddy and Donnie: siblings, to be sure, but in nature and temperament so very different, with Willie himself falling somewhere in between the two. At the time that he is now recalling, the brothers had been evacuated from their home in Glasgow to the care of their maternal grandparents on Skye - for the duration of the Second World War.

It was a move that hadn't suited Roddy. Ambitious and restless of spirit, he is a city boy, through and through. He misses the city bustle, the tenements and the territorial battles of the slum back alleys, misses the child gangs, misses being a member of a like-minded mob, while aspiring to becoming its ultimate leader. The countryside bores and disgusts him. The croft animals - cows sheep horses hens - smelly and dumb, are everywhere, openly, and as the notion takes them, crapping all over the landscape!

Also, he can't understand how his younger brothers can find hours of amusement from splashing around in the river; find amusement from pieces of wood and stone, which they imagine to be ships and buses and cars. They are only what they are, for Pete's sake(!)- silly bits of wood and stone! Even *shennair's* ghost stories bore Roddy - or so he will claim! His wide eyes, though, flashing in the darkened, flame flickering room suggests otherwise!

Little Donnie, on the other hand, is totally different. Artistic and poetic and sensitive, there is an eternal stillness about Donnie. Even back then, as a child, he senses and loves the romance and pastoral spirituality of Gaeldom. Tragedy or misfortune, however, especially for people close to him, deeply affect him. The imminent early death of their father, and the subsequent hardship of their mother's widowhood, he will find particularly hard to take. And in such situations, when he finds that he can't be of any help, in order to cope, he retreats into this personal sanctuary of his – a mystical spiritual stillness. In Willie's eyes, Donnie was capable of becoming a poet, a prophet, a mystic, and because of that, he was proud of him, almost in awe of him, and loved him deeply.

Returning to the present, and dozing off again on the waves of his reminiscences, words stir in the deep stores of Willie's mind: not other men's words this time, - the 'other men's words' he had told Cathy on the train about - but his own words, for he *did* have them, words formulated some time ago in the Glasgow flat. It had been during a particularly bad time, a low time of heavy drinking and emotional darkness. He had scribbled the words down in the wee small hours as they had come to him. He can't decipher the drunken scribbles next day, but no matter, the words are so lodged in his mind he remembers them anew, in the form of a disturbing poem:

> *It was something black awoke me,*
>
> *And my eyes snapped open wide:*
>
> *I heard the wind that haunts the moor*
>
> *And the crashing of the tide.*

*That something black, it made me rise,*
*From a soft and warm bed:*
*The woman groaned, still half asleep*
*Don't go! Don't go! she said.*

*But I stepped out in the icy blast,*
*The wind screeched round my head:*
*Storm clouds raced across the moon*
*And the river it ran red.*

*I saw the tracks of cloven hoofs,*
*Sensed mortal veneers fall:*
*And heard the shrill demonic laugh*
*And the banshee whispers call...*

*... Oh Lord! ... the banshee whispers call!*

Oh yes, not just other men's words, he had his own words also, dark words perhaps, words that must say something about him.

And along with his words, he has his memories – so many memories. Memories! How many memories can a man store away? . . . amazing, mundane, wonderful, terrible things . . . and being back in Skye, it is memories of the old Gaelic *Black Houses* that come to him now! . . .

Yes, the *Black Houses of Gaeldom:* it is hard to believe that they were being used for human habitation well into the twentieth century. Primitive and unsanitary, they had housed, un-evolving, the Gaels of Scotland and of Ireland for centuries.

After surviving for so long, their disappearance would be rapid, melting away as they had, like ghosts - banished back, suddenly unwanted, to the earth from where they had sprung. Those that did remain, remained as inexorably vanishing ruins….. remote…. half hidden by untended heath…… lifeless and un-needed, unappreciated, suddenly unloved - ghost-ridden and resentful; dark-brooding and unwelcoming now - guarding their old stories and ancient secrets

Unbelievably, Willie himself has memories of families who had actually lived in the Black Houses - memories of visiting them, as a young child, with his mother. . .

*The walls are made of rough stones and rocks, sometimes even clods of earth. The roofs, supported by undressed tree beams or rafters, are clad by reeds and rushes, or heather, or, again, clods of earth. During heavy rain, there are invariably leaks - the* sileadh.

*There is a central external entrance, leading to two main chambers. The chamber to the left is for storage and the wintering of animals, principally a cow or two, and sometimes a horse. The chamber to the right is for the humans. In the darkness, the differing species can hear the others shift position, cough, snore, breathe, fart. Primitive conditions indeed.*

*The fire is positioned in the middle of the floor, directly beneath a hole in the thatched roof. The hole is meant to take the smoke away. It is far from effective and thick peat smoke constantly pervades the interior - dark-staining human faces.*

*This particular day, as usual, the younger and more able family members are busy with outside chores. The ageing grandmother and grandfather – the 'cailleach' and the 'bodach',- remain inside, chatting with the child Willie and his mother. They are all sitting around the open peat fire.*

*A scallywag of about twelve, one of the bored family youngsters, clambers up the thatch with a jug of water and pours the contents down the hole. There is sudden mayhem below - demented hissing, wild sparks, cursing, shrieking, old people falling backwards off their stools.*

*Something should be down about that scallywag!*

*Only the previous week, he had filled his grand-mother's freshly emptied chamber pot with a liberal helping of 'Andrew's Liver Salts' - a self medicating particularly popular 'pick-me-up' of the time, and comprising of a crystalline powder that is subject to violent effervescence on contact with anything liquid.*

*Grandmother's resultant night-time yells - piteous and high pitched - will subsequently alarm nearby human and beast alike.*

*Strangulation will later be mooted, as a possible cure for the scallywag!*

Yes, memories! - memories, set in motion and piling, one upon another, now . . .

*He is around ten years old and visiting cousins, who live some seven miles from home.*

*Time passes. Reluctantly, he must leave - mustn't get caught by the dark. But on the way back, there are distractions - scattered neighbours he hasn't seen for a while; and there is the postman's brand-new mail van; and an interesting unexplored river.*

*Belatedly, he becomes aware of the advancing darkness. And there is still the bleak three mile stretch of the Vatten moorland road to go. And Gaeldom is awash with ghosts, fairies and spirits - good and evil - deep entrenched in its soul and in its legends.*

*It's the evil spirits that spring to his mind now, especially the particular one said to haunt the night-time Vatten Moor, the very road he is now travelling, a spirit roaming in the guise of an old man wearing a white coat.*

*His hair begins to stand on end. But he must remain strong - mustn't give way to childish fear!*

*YAHHHH! Suddenly he sees the old man! . . . But wait! No! It's only a rock!*

*YAHHHH! Now he sees him for real... But wait again! No! It's only a sheep - in the darkness, very similar to an old man in a white coat! And there are rocks and sheep suddenly everywhere. Cold shivers on his spine and with his head pounding, he begins to run - his pace steadily increasing as he goes.*

*They say it is the roads that the old man trawls. Right - he will cut across the moor! But the old man and the sheep and the rocks are still there, all around him - everywhere!. He has never experienced such cold terror in all of his life. He breasts the brow of the hill and sees the faint outline of his grand-parents' house in the glen floor below. It spurs him on*

*He is running so fast now his feet are hardly touching the ground. He doesn't know how he does it in the dim moon light - how he doesn't break a leg, the rough ground consisting as it does of rock, clump of heather and slippery peat slime.*

*With the old man closing in, he reaches the boundary barbed wire fence, slides under the lowest strand and is back on his feet again without stopping. He crashes through the door into the darkened interior of the house.*

*Familiar smells…. familiar sounds…. familiar shadows.*

*He is safe!!*

Totally awake finally, he realises he is still exhausted and again profusely perspiring, the eating beast again stirring within him - relentlessly gnawing… gnawing.

He gazes up at the skylight window, framing a small square patch of sky, yet black and frosty starred, through which, as a child, he had so often witnessed the dawns and deaths of days that were grand and days that were terrible - the dawns and deaths of seasons long vanished.

He remembers himself and his brothers back then, standing on the bed in order to raise the glass and peer out across the eye-level slated roof, smelling the peat scented air and hearing the shoosh of the river in the floor of the glen. If the night is moonlit, they can see the river's winding course and the vague outline of silvery fields, the latter seemingly peopled by shuffling shadows - ghosts - indefinable shadows that are up to no good! At this point, increasingly afraid, they slam the skylight window shut and dive back under the covers. Laughingly, although they dare never actually laugh about it, it is invariably an ashen faced Roddy who will instigate the move, being the first to collapse back on the bed and grab the lion's share of the reassuring blankets.

The memory fading, Willie realises that the wind of earlier has died and a soft calm has settled on the morning. Lying motionless, breathing slowly, he listens to the river, and the occasional forlorn bleat of hill sheep. How very different, the world out there, to the one beyond the window of his Glasgow flat.

After a seeming eternity of time, there is a pearly greying in the eastern sky and on cue the old croft rooster scratches himself awake and crows his self-important call, preparing himself for another day of strutting as he establish his dunged domain - and all to impress his ladies! The thought of the pompous old fellow makes Willie smile.

The dawn light increases further and his eyes move to the wall, to the framed photograph that is yellowed with age. The photograph conveys some long past harvest scene: a blistering hot day, with a group of crofter men and women arrayed around a horse and cart laden with hay. There are a couple of tentative smiles. Some have adopted vain, self-conscious poses for the rare photographic occasion, but mostly the camera is being regarded with grim suspicion. It is a very old photograph, and Willie's eye runs along the faded faces - broad Gaelic faces. What hopes, what dreams were there? Possibly, some of them spoke only the Gaelic. Undoubtedly, they were now all dead, the already disintegrating remnants of a once proud and prolific warrior race. Yes indeed, what of their dreams? How long had they lived? To what part of the globe had they fled? Had Fate been kind? He imagines their hopeful voices echoing down the petrified years - mildewed and meaningless now, like their images on the wall.

Finlay has his breakfast already on the table when he walks into the kitchen and is as bright and breezy and healthy as a fine summer's day, appearing to be suffering no ill effects from the over-indulgences of the previous evening.

Following breakfast, Finlay is anxious to show Willie his cattle, which he proceeds to do with the justifiable pride of a doting father. After all, Finlay considers his cattle to be his family, his babies, and Willie experiences a pang of regret; after all, he too has an inbred affection for croft animals, having a special affinity with the cows - fellow travelers on the hard journey of living from the land, indispensable allies and companions in the fight for rural survival. Their scent, the warmth of their breath, the smell of their stalls, the dark sweaty ambience of the byre, are memories – deep rooted.

Holding a flickering storm lantern aloft as a boy, assisting his grandfather at times of sickness and difficult calvings, he has shared in their trials and intimate triumphs. He remembers them all, from his earliest remembrance, not as collective long-gone shadows but as individual cows, individual characters - their names, their appearances, their foibles, the turn of their gentle enquiring eyes. He has carried their memory in a silent inner place, into distant city exile - vivid memories, half a century old.


By mid-morning he decides to leave Finlay to his work, while he himself browses around the croft – a trip down memory lane. It is the weekend and the murderous police business that has brought him to Skye can wait until Monday. Finlay suggests that he takes one of the collies for company.

'Take Dan. Daft as a brush, eh? Will go with anyone who will throw him a stick. Disloyal brute. Don't know why I bother to keep and feed him, eh?' Finlay chuckles, not meaning that. 'Old Bess now is a different kettle of fish. Only her death will drag old Bess from my side.'

Leaving Finlay to his chores, Willie and a stick-chasing Dan wander down a well-worn path through the fields, passing the family's former source of drinking water on the way - the old sweet watered natural spring.

Ignoring brother Roddy's disdain, how many times had he and brother Donnie trod this path as children, playing at being buses or lorries, the illusion enhanced by loud *broom-brooms* and the furious changing of imaginary gears.

At the path's end is the river, seemingly eternal and so much part of childhood, with its dark peat stained waters - waters which have reflected countless passing moons, and a legion vanished faces.

Reaching the salmon pool, he recalls pitch black nights, with silent poaching men, crouched breathless and anciently aroused as they draw in the splash-nets - nets heavy with their bounty of thrashing silver.

He throws the inexhaustible Dan another stick.

Moving slowly on, he arrives at the old wooden bridge leading to the peat track on the opposite moor. It has long collapsed, its timber piers rotted now and clawed by nettles. The peat track itself snakes on, up the opposite hill, through a maze of heather, bracken and bog-land, skirting the ruins of a *Black House* - a forlorn accusing relic from the time of *The Clearances*.

And another childhood memory comes to him; how so often, at the corner of his eye, he had fancied furtive movement at these ruins - tormented shadows - as if his ancestors were coming at him, flapping and shuffling, not with hostility or ill-intent; merely claiming him as kin, but yet sending him fleeing with cold shivers on his spine.

Throwing yet another stick for Dan, he stops by the pool where the children had swam and bathed on hot summer days, and where the gossiping women had stone-washed the clothes. His thoughts drifting, he recalls their Gaelic songs and their laughter, hanging on warm heather-scented breezes.

Dan cocks his head to one side, yellow eyes bright with anticipation.

*When is this fellow going to pay attention and throw another stick!*

Self-engrossed, Willie moves on, arriving eventually at the furthermost boundary of the family croft, where the fence is in a bad state of repair, the timber posts angled, the barbed wire rusted and sagging.

Nearby, is the communal crofting sheep fank, evidently still in use. Feeling the need of a rest now, he leans against its wooden rails and glances west. Fifty yards further on is the stone bridge that carries the main road over the river, its single arch framing the distant sea loch beyond, fingering inland from the Atlantic. Breathing deeply, he feels the tang of pure sea air seeping to the bottom of his lungs - a deeply pleasurable sensation, reminding him how good it is to be alive.

His eyes wander to the grassy bank on the sheltered, landward side of the stone bridge and known in the old days as The Knoll. The Knoll has always had great significance in his memory. He has thought about it, and dreamt about it, often over the years. Even as he had set out with Dan on his present wander, he had thought of it with warm anticipation - as a highlight.

The Knoll had been a traditional camping site for the wandering tinker clans of his childhood. And how could one ever forget the tinkers, with their ancient bow tents? There had been different feuding clans of them. Fierce, wild eyed people, untamed and ever ready for battle, governed it seemed in those days by no laws but their own unavoidable laws of survival - the laws of quick wit and an even quicker fist. Horse traders they had been mostly, and the menders of pots and pans; restless and wandering - always wandering.

There had been black and red headed clans of them. As a child, it had been the black ones had overawed him the most, had been the ones he secretly hero worshipped - so loud, vital and outrageous. A large number of the old crofters had feared the tinkers, not just their fighting men but also their women, their clay-pipe smoking women, with their powers of the *evil eye*. Many were the tales of those who had upset the tinkers and had been cursed by the *evil eye,* their crops becoming fallow and their cows running dry.

Remaining against the sheep fank rail, he wonders about the unjust misconceptions that occur in life, for hadn't the general population of those unenlightened days not been brainwashed into believing of the tinkers as parasites and thieves, little better than vermin; a belief persistently instilled in an uneducated people by Tory landlordism and for the purposes of protecting southern interests: *gun-fodder for the Empire's jolly old wars, or dancing at the end of a rope is the only fitting destiny for the bounders!*

How chillingly unjust he had subsequently discovered these misconceptions to be as he was to learn, on the contrary, that the tinkers were born from a sense of independence; from a fierce freedom of the spirit. Unwilling to submit to the thankless drudgery of working land that could never be theirs, refusing to be beholden to any man, far less an unjustly privileged master, theirs had been a way of free living and unfettered wandering stretching back to the mists of a distant Celtic dawn.

His eyes rest on The Knoll now, and Rosie-Anne's image comes to him - as he had known in advance that it must. Rosie-Anne has come to him in his dreams many times over the years. It is the memory of Rosie-Anne has given The Knoll its greatest significance for him.

He is around eleven years old when he first sets eyes upon her. The Glasgow schools being closed for the summer vacation, he is back with his grandparents on Skye for the duration. Spotting her shortly after his arrival, he has gazed fixedly upon her on many occasions, but only from a distance, fascinated by her bronze skin and long raven black hair as she moves around the tinkers' camp with the arrogant grace of a cat - and he has become besotted. It is approaching high noon of a blistering-hot airless Sunday, when he eventually meets her face to face.

Alone and keeping an eye on the animals while the rest of the family are at church, he sees her padding towards him along the old dirt road. His grandfather has set aside a jug of milk on the doorstep; *'should the tinkers be needing some'*.

She is casually swinging a tin can, attached to a wire handle, as she approaches. At around fourteen years of age, she towers over him, her penetrating black eyes slightly mocking, her shoulder length hair hanging loose and unruly.

'Hello, me lad, it's meself be Rosie-Anne. I've come for a droppie o' milk. Are the old folks around?

She is bare footed and wearing a thin floral summer frock, an obvious hand-me-down that's at least a size too small for her, the taut material clinging to her lithe perspiring body. She notices his eyes fixated on her firm sprouting breasts. Already instinctively worldly-wise, and increasingly aware of her emerging female 'powers', she smiles knowingly.

'Haven't seen ye around the place before, me lad. Be ye kin?'

'I'm a grandson. I used to live here. I'm up on school holiday from Glasgow. They are all off to church. I'm looking after the place.'

Her dark eyes bore down upon him - amused. 'All on yer own me lad?' Spotting the milk jug on the doorstep with a protective plate placed on top, she moves forward and transfers the contents to her tin can. As she brushes past him, and despite her perspiration, he catches a brief whiff of pleasant scent - the scent of fresh soap and cool mountain water.

'It's a big place to be lookin' after on yer own, me lad. A man's job. And yerself be yet but a wee boy'

Bristling uncomfortably, he responds. 'I'm not a wee boy!'

Her eyes sweeping him up and down, she smiles some more and pulls at the frock material adhering to her skin

'Phew! Jaysus! Must be the hottest day o' the summer.' Sitting down on a grass bank by the side of the dirt road, she pats the ground beside her.

'Here, me lad, sit down. Be tellin' me all about yerself.'

He sits down, but opposite her, on the other side of the road. Her smile widens and then she laughs scornfully. 'Ye wouldn't be afraid o' me now, would ye? Aye, yer yet but a wee boy, sure enough!'

They gaze at one another across the still air and the midday furnace heat. Nothing stirs. The only sound comes from the river, and from the hum of a bumble bee flitting among the heather blooms. Rosie-Anne pulls her knees up towards her chest, her legs a fraction apart, and his eyes are immediately and unavoidably drawn towards the dark mystery of her crotch.

Gasping for air, it begins to dawn on him: that on this momentous day, Rosie-Anne has omitted, or has forgotten, to wear her drawers!

The intensity of the heat, incredibly, seems to increase, the very ground now threatening to split asunder. The bee has found a bounty of nectar and is momentarily silent. The entire universe, indeed, appears to have fallen suddenly silent, the only sound now coming solely from the river - the timeless river, washing its ancient stones. In the soundless vacuum of heat, it seems so unusually loud.

He and Rosie-Anne are now the only inhabitants of the universe - and time stands still.

Exhilarated by Willie's obvious arousal, and carried along by these emerging 'powers' of hers, Rosie-Anne fractionally widens the spread of her legs. And she too is now breathing more heavily, because she instinctively knows that she is playing an ancient and potentially dangerous game - she is playing with fire and could get badly burned. And only she will be to blame! All of it will be her fault! She is the female, after all - the temptress, leading him on. Her sisters, since Eve and from time immemorial, could warn her about that. Even today, in certain parts of the world, she could be put to death!

But she is young, wild and free, and experimentation is hard to avoid or resist. She has to find these things out for herself. The spirited young have to challenge old taboos. It is a rite of passage. But yes, a dangerous game! And then, the adults could return at any moment from church and catch her out, realise what mischief she is up to.

All the while, Willie's eyes remain fixated on the hypnotic dark mass – fascinating but, across the width of the dirt road, frustratingly vague and undefined - mysterious . . . taunting . . . beckoning . . . highly exciting . . . but, to a young lad, so very frightening at the same time!

His breathing becomes non-existent, he is in turmoil, his head spinning, his body wracked by unfamiliar stirrings - burning, new and wonderful sensations.

Transfixed and trapped, he begins to panic. What he is doing is evil! He has learned that much at church. It is a mortal sin, they had preached - ogling at, lusting after a female's naked bits! He tries to look away but can't. On the contrary, he is desiring closer scrutiny, desiring contact - physical exploration - looking away is an impossibility.

Rosie-Anne's legs snap suddenly shut. Crimson faced, he glances up. The conqueror, smiling triumphantly, rises to her feet and gazes back down at the conquered.

'Aye, just a wee boy, to be sure' she says, and begins to walk away.

After a few steps, she stops and turns her head around, her wild hair hiding one eye. 'Be sure to be thankin' yer folks for the milk now.'

Lying crumpled on the side of the road, Willie hasn't moved, his face still crimson, and Rosie-Anne feels a pang of conscience. The boy isn't alone, she realises, for she too can feel a flush of red on her face.

'Perhaps I was wrong, me lad, perhaps ye aren't a wee boy at all. Not yet a man either, mind ye, but perhaps not that very far off it. Me thinks I could even be getting tae likin' ye one day.' Laughing then, still slightly mockingly, she tosses her head, to flick the hair away from her eye, and swinging her milk can and her hips, she heads back down the old dirt road, with that feline walk of hers.

Unmoving, Willie watches her go, watches her until she vanishes beyond the crest of the hill - and feeling more besotted than ever by her.

He could easily have felt crushed and humiliated, destroyed, but what she had said there at the end had made everything just fine. Yes, besotted by her he is, and he now deeply yearns for her to stay - stay forever by his side. But he is never to see her up close again. It will be one of her many siblings will fetch the milk in future. And then one morning, away before dawn and without warning, her clan breaks camp and are gone. Every day after that, for the remainder of the school holidays, he will visit that Knoll, the lush grassy bank where her camp had been - distraught with longing, sensing her presence.

Returning to the present and the company of Dan, Willie smiles wistfully at the memory.

Gazing though the arch of the stone bridge, to the sea loch beyond, he remembers the flask of whisky in his hip pocket. It had been given to him by Finlay - in case he should feel the cold during his walk. But he has done well, hasn't touched a drop until now. Unscrewing the lid, he raises the flask to his lips and downs a good half of it in one swallow, enjoying the liquid warming his insides.

Remaining motionless, he feels the sudden rise of a cool breeze on his face, coming towards him unbroken from the sea loch, a soft sigh, indolent, in no hurry, caressing his cheek. Savouring the moment, he closes his eyes and hears the stirrings of gently mocking laughter. His eyes snap open as he listened more closely . . .

 . . . but the laughter has gone, the only sound now being the breeze's own whisperings in the long grass. And then the breeze itself dies as quickly as it had risen, and he glances across to The Knoll and knows that it had been Rosie-Anne. She hadn't been there in person, of course, but her spirit had been there - had never been away. And Rosie-Anne's spirit had been calling to him just then, just as the spirits of his ancestors had done so often at the Black House ruins.

# LIFT ME, DADDY

The euphoric effects of the whisky are washing over him, and the smile he is smiling widens, for he is gladdened by what he has just experienced. City folks wouldn't understand such things - such things as vanished voices and old laughter in the wind. Indeed, they would have guffawed with scornful derision.

Alex Craig would have wet himself!

You had to be a Gael, a Celt, to understand. You had to be a child of the peat fires, the oil lamps and the flickering shadows; a child steeped in the soil, in the handed down ghost stories, a child conversant with blasted moorland, with howling Atlantic winds and long and black banshee winter nights.

Dan, meantime, has given up on the hope of chasing sticks. He is lying down now, his head resting on his paws but his yellow eyes flicking occasionally open - just in case!

The eating beast stirs anew, deep within Willie's insides and he slumps against one of the sheep shearing banks. Placing his head in his hands, a chill sweat rises on his brow. The spasm of pain eventually eases and he raises his eyes. The watery winter sun has sailed westwards and in the distance he can see the old family house - Finlay's house now: its lime washed walls pristine white against the shadow of the hill, it is so totally different from city houses, having pretensions to neither status nor show; essentially a protection against the elements. Simple, humble, it is a beacon of family, of refuge - *'home'* in the truest sense. Although not so ground-rooted as the older Black Houses, it is still very much *'of'* the land rather than being merely cast upon it.

His eyes swing on beyond the house, along a two mile range of hill, picking up a receding string of scattered similar houses - white jewels in the setting sun.

'All of these houses, Dan. And all of their original Gaelic people gone, every single one! To God knows where.....'

Not too optimistically, Dan opens one eye. Sticks!

'......the McLeods, the McRaes, the Camerons, the Nicholsons, the MacKays, the McSweens. All of them gone! It's the Ludgroves, the Winterbottoms, the Bradshaws, the Platts, the Balls are there now.'

Late afternoon shadows are visibly fingering down the crofts, down fields that are blackened by the ravages of winter, derelict of crops, empty of people. He remembers them alive with the bustle and the Gaelic voices of harvesters, as neighbouring families pulled together in communal effort and assistance - a time of hard physical toil, admittedly, but a time of joyous laughter also. A time for maids and youths to meet and flirt, dreaming of romance, love ever-lasting, and the making of new generations - new Gaelic generations! What unbearable emptiness and loneliness lie on these same fields now - '*the mute regret of sunlit gravestones*'.

The vivid mental imagery of the day's reminiscences, the realisation that he has been dallying with an absent and banished people, dallying with but ghosts, is suddenly all too much. He drops his head in his hands again, silently weeping.

And Dan raises his head from his paws, cocks it to one side, yellow eyes wide and enquiring. A big handsome dog, he has the high intelligence of his collie breed. You could be excused for believing that he understood.

## SIX

By the following Monday, Willie has gathered himself together to concentrate on the murder investigations which have brought him to Skye. And for the subsequent five days, he consults with both sergeant McRae, the locally based police officer, as well as with detective constable McLean from Highland Division HQ in Inverness.

While bearing in mind that all murder victims have been English, painstaking door to door investigations have produced little information, other than what is already common knowledge; namely, that there is an air of general disquiet among the indigenous populace over the ever increasing waves of southern immigration - to the Highlands in general, and to the Hebridean islands in particular. All in all, the reaction is no more than that - disquiet, accompanied by grumblings and mutterings - a far cry from inexcusable hatred and murder.

The Gaels being, by nature, a welcoming and hospitable race, it isn't the immigration or the nationality of the immigrants that bothers them, but the swamping extent of that immigration. There isn't only the question of house prices rising beyond the reach of local Gaels, which is particularly problematic for the young setting off on married life, but there is also the question of the Gaels being outnumbered, swamped, and eventually marginalised, with the resultant threat to their language and culture. Had the situation been reversed, no doubt the immigrants would have experienced identical misgivings and concerns in respect of the identical adverse effects on *their* country, language and culture.

Willie himself has to admit to sharing in the general feeling of disquiet, a fact which, considering his many close English friends and his genuine admiration of the traditional English culture and character, gives him cause for some guilt. His attraction to fellow beings has never been based on their race, colour or beliefs, but on their level of humanity.

The killer, meantime, has been careful to leave no apparent physical clues as to his identity, there being no fingerprints, only one shoeprint, found beside the victim at Kelvingrove Park in Glasgow.

Detective constable McLean had recently read about a new system being developed called 'DNA Profiling' which, it was reckoned, would replace fingerprints and would be potentially more conclusive, but this breakthrough is still in its infancy and apparently some years in the future.

In the interests of doing 'something constructive' however, Sgt McRae has taken the initiative of compiling a list of locals and of traceable non-locals who regularly commute from Skye to Glasgow and vice versa, such as travelling salesmen, delivery van drivers and the like, with a view to matching their movements with the times of the murders in the two locations. It is a long shot and a daunting undertaking, but a beginning has to be made somewhere. The killer, it could reasonably be assumed, would be Skye or Glasgow based. Sgt McRae's list of names will initially be confined to the area of the island known as 'The Peninsula', based on the fact that all of the victims had resided or owned property there. It could also to be assumed, under the circumstances, that the killer is a Gael, although this is no watertight certainty.

And then, of course, there are the riddles and the single letters of signature, which have been pored over and dissected and discussed without any definite conclusions having been reached. And with that, the murder investigation grinds to a, hopefully temporary halt.

In the meantime, a relative of Willies, a grand aunt, dies while he is on the island and he attends her funeral the day before his return to Glasgow. The relative, Maggie McQueen, is a sister of his maternal grandmother. The funeral takes place in 'The Peninsula', the ancestral lands of the McQueens.

Old Maggie McQueen is one hundred and two when she passes on, her mental faculties yet sharp, her spirit undiminished. It is said that her physical body simply couldn't keep pace and died around her. Old Maggie had been a bit of a Gaelic institution - the end of an era. Born and raised in a *Black House,* she had childhood memories of *The Clearances;* had relatives who had died at The Battle of Waterloo, the Indian Mutiny and in the Boer War. Her own brother had been a leading light in the Land League Battles, fighting for crofters' rights. The end of an era indeed, and Willie had felt a sense of privilege by his attendance at her funeral, the service for which had been conducted at her home, the vast number of mourners over-spilling into the garden.

The men had been bare headed as they bowed to the prayers of the Free Presbyterian minister. Surveying them, Willie had noted that most of them were balding, were white haired - were old. It had been difficult to believe that they were the broken remnants of a proud once warrior race, their broad boned and red skinned faces being reflections of their Gaelic brothers in Ireland. How sad, he had thought, that history and distance had parted and weakened them, how absurd that the blight of religious bigotry had divided them.

The prayers had been followed by the singing of Gaelic psalms, the mournful cadences of the discordant unaccompanied voices being anciently beautiful, indigenous and timeless, drifting across the wintery sea loch. Relays of mourners had then carried Old Maggie on their shoulders to her last resting place, a preceding piper playing the haunting lament, *The Flowers of The Forest.* Her allocated plot, the last to be occupied in a very old Gaelic cemetery, was a weed strewn swath of green, a crumbling stone wall cradling it from the encroachment of surrounding sea and heather-clad hill.

Beyond the rattle of frosted earth falling on the coffin and breaking a vast winter silence, Willie had fancied he heard a collective sigh from the very land and its myriad creatures, and from the mist-hidden ghosts of a legion dead ancestors.

And with his rejoicing at the last goodbye afforded Old Maggie - for she had been buried with the grace of the queen she had undoubtedly been, and with the reverence due the last of a spent generation - he couldn't but think of Donnie, his younger brother Donnie, lying, in comparison, in a vandalised and soot engrained city cemetery in distant turbulent Glasgow. Lying among strangers.

It was of some significance that old Maggie's funeral had taken place on 'The Peninsula', in so far as the area had become a 'hot-spot' in the Riddle Killings investigations, all of the victims having had some form of connections there.

The Peninsula itself had a rather grim history, having been particularly targeted by *The Clearances*, with their associated injustice and atrocity. As in many places in the Highlands and islands, *The Clearances* had required that the indigenous Gaelic peoples be 'cleared' from their land in order to make way for the lucrative business of rearing sheep, (later, by the creation of sporting estates), the land then being subdivided among a few privileged individuals, a large number of whom being from England.

As was the case elsewhere, the '*cleared*' Gaels of The Peninsula, having had their few possessions confiscated and their homes burned, were often required to survive on the rocky shoreline, sometimes being reduced to eating seaweed.

The result was that many of these Gaelic victims, in desperation, took advantage of 'free passage' on emigration ships, to mainly America, Canada and the Antipodes, the 'free passage' being, in some few instances, instigated by humane Scottish benefactors, but on the whole the emigration programme was a Central Government ruse to rid itself of a difficult and 'inconvenient' problem, a ruse designed to have the unwanted victim 'wretches' do just that - emigrate! GO!

Adding to the resultant misery and gloom descending at the time upon The Peninsula, the Free Presbyterian church tightens its grip, imposing a severe doom-laden fundamental religious doctrine. This doctrine, in truth, may have given solace to those individuals left bereft of any possession hope and purpose, but its insistence that enjoying oneself is evil: - *no singing, no dancing, no alcohol, no being frivolously happy* - instills an all-consuming air of apathy and resigned hopelessness.

Adding to it all, there are the colonial wars that will decimate the remaining Gaelic male population still further. These wars are followed by the Great Wars of 1914 and 1945. In the course of the 1914 war in particular, the Gaels are, per capita, to suffer the highest casualty figures within the entire British commonwealth, and following which, having been conditioned into actually believing it by their own political leadership, Englishmen will persistently declare that it was '*England won the war*' And for countless years thereafter, hurt and offended Gaels, men women and children, will make the protest: *Oh, really? Only England?*

Similarly, other participation nations, on the allies' side, are airbrushed out. The news agencies of the time will invariably report that great advances are being made by 'England' and by 'English soldiers'. Equally, setbacks and terrible slaughter are reported as being suffered again by 'England' and by 'English' soldiers.

It is an insensitive and ignorant arrogance that belittles and dismisses other people's beloved nations and nationality; an arrogance that diminishes and dismisses other people's slaughter, sorrow and sacrifice. There are instances of aged Gaelic parents left to tackle the physical hardship of their crofts and livelihoods alone, while four or five sons are enlisted to fight, and die - pleas to have at least one son spared for home duties, having fallen on deaf ears. And then there will be receipt of the dreaded telegrams, the death notices from the War Office - thousands upon thousands of them - a never ending stream: *'It is my painful duty to inform you…'*

It is a pain and injustice that cuts deep. And pain injustice and insult can be enduring - and memories can be long!

Existing and evolving within the mayhem and misery of these dark times is the predominant 'peninsula' clan - the McQueens - their experiences and lot resulting in an amazing mish-mash of individuals - from the artistic and highly intelligent, who will make their mark in many parts of the world, to the reclusive, the inbred and the mad. Many of Old Maggie's generation, as is the case with herself, will remain unmarried and, as a result, that branch of the McQueen clan will largely die out.

In the latter respect, The Great World Wars again don't help, with so many men being killed off, leaving the womenfolk bereft of partners; *'Who is going to give us our children?'* being a common and heart-rending female lament of the time.

Old Maggie's own sister, the neurotic and highly over-sexed Polly, will be tragically affected by the situation. If she is to meet the mate she is so desperately and forever seeking, she will require to leave The Peninsula - possibly the entire Highlands. But this she cannot do. Being the eldest child, after Maggie, and with the menfolk away, she has the croft to look after, in addition to aged parents and several younger siblings. The bliss of a loving husband and treasured children is apparently beyond Polly's reach - is but a hollow dream.

The situation drives Polly into deep depression. She no longer thinks in a rational fashion. The signs are that over-sexed Polly McQueen will never sample the joy of life's sweetest wine. It's all so terribly cruel - so terribly unjust!

Polly McQueen's health suffers.

Polly McQueen begins to lose her mind.

But Polly hangs on and grows older.

The aged parents eventually die: A brother matures and takes over the running of the croft. Younger sisters, Rachel and Effie, mature also, and Polly decides she is no longer needed.

Having prepared the evening meal for her brother and other siblings as usual, and having meticulously set the table, Polly brushes back her greying coal black hair, carefully places her favourite Sunday hat on top, laces up her 'special occasion' shoes and pulls on her coat. She then walks calmly away from the house, unseen; walks purposefully across the moors towards the high cliffs of the headlands - and leaps silently into the sea.

It had been a dreadful period in Gaelic history, and standing alone at old Maggie's grave now, the last to leave her internment, Willie pushes the thought of it from his mind. He is glad that sergeant McRae has afforded him the use of an unmarked police car. It gives him freedom of movement.

Old Maggie's burial done and dusted, he had bidden farewell to relations and friends, declining an invitation to the post burial gathering at the nearby hotel. Waiting at the latter would be the customary food and refreshment and, more significantly from Willie's point of view, the traditional alcoholic toasts - which carried a distinct risk of him overdoing things and 'letting the side down'! In the meantime, his craving for whisky has been worsening as the day progresses, his will power to resist increasingly weakening. Even now at the cemetery gates, his hand is already beginning to shake, his desire for a drink sharpening. He is also experiencing stabs of internal physical pain. Easing into the unmarked car, he turns his head and watches the cars of fellow mourners streaming along the road, heading for the hotel.

# LIFT ME, DADDY

He wonders who owns the hotel these days.

In the mid-fifties, during holiday trips from Glasgow, he and brother Donnie would often frequent that same hotel. It was the De Grootes, a Dutch family, who owned it back then. Located in the middle of the severe Presbyterian ambiance of The Peninsula, it had served as a magnet for the rebellious local young.

Johann De Groote, an atheist, firmly believed that hotels were created for pleasure and fun, and to this end he regularly arranged for dances and ceilidhs to be held in his premises - *'Let's dance at De Groote, he don't give a hoot!'*, being the chant from not only the local 'Peninsula' young, but also from others across the island.

Recalling one memorable après-ceilidh incident, a wistful look comes into Willie's expression: At the time, he owned a French car, known as the Citroen 'Light Fifteen.' A sleek, low-slung car with flared mudguards and large chrome headlights, it is renowned for its road holding capabilities.

His thoughts drift back:

*The ceilidh is over and the De Groote Hotel in semi-darkness, when Willie and Donnie are spotted entering the Citroen by an aged and very inebriated kilted bagpiper, who is accompanied by two equally aged and inebriated companions. The bedraggled trio had earlier contributed to the ceilidh's entertainment, in that the piper had piped and one of the companions had sung Gaelic songs - with his 'wonderful singing voice'. The second companion had also sung Gaelic songs with what he - and he alone(!) - considered to be a 'wonderful singing voice'.*

*The trio are now searching for a 'lift home'.*

*The kilted piper had arrived at the ceilidh with his pipes in their purpose-made storage box. But, with the ceilidh over, the box is nowhere to be found, and the pipes are now clasped under his arm. Addressing the shadows in the Citroen, he enquires if 'a lift home' might be a possibility - 'home' being a small crofting community called 'Far Flung' and located five miles distant at the end of a single-track dirt road.*

*Willie's slurred voice expansively assures the trio, from the vicinity of the driver's seat: 'No, gentlemen, it won't be a possibility at all, it will*

Iain Ferguson

*be an absolute certainty - and a pleasure and an honour to boot! Get in! Get in!'*

*Equally as inebriated as his prospective passengers, Willie is slumped sideways as he endeavours to locate the elusive hole into which one is meant to insert an ignition key.*

*Whooping with gratitude and delight, the three old timers, plus a set of bagpipes, clamber into the rear of the car.*

*The elusive hole discovered, the engine is fired up.*

*Cock-eyed, Willie regards his passengers in his rear-view mirror while addressing them with a rather perplexing announcement: 'Right! Here we go boys! Are you ready! Hold on tightly to your hats!' Despite their state of inebriation, it is an announcement which the old timers find mildly disturbing.*

*Slipping the car into gear then, Willie presses down on the accelerator and the vehicle leaps forward into the night. Turning into the dirt road, he now pushes the accelerator all the way to the floorboards, the sudden increase in speed pushing the old timers, and the bagpipes, into the far depths of the rear seats. Reaching a hummock on the road, the Citroen rises up on her suspension, threatening to take flight, then dives downward and bottoms out into the hollow that follows. The hollow, in turn, is followed by the comparative calm of a short straight stretch of road before the arrival of a series of bends, when the car slews left, then slews right, then right again, skidding sideways, tyres screeching and sending an arc of dust and gravel fanning outward into the adjoining moor. All the while, the Citroen's headlight beams probe upwards into the night sky, then bore down into the bowels of the earth, then sweep across the landscape - left, right, left, left again, right.*

*And now - Holy Moses! - there is yet another series of humps and hollows and sharp bends fast approaching them in the road ahead!*

*In the back of the car by now, a tangled mass of old timers - along with bagpipes - have slipped from the rear seat onto the floor, rapidly sobering up and piteously screaming:*

*'We are going to die! We are going to die! Stop the car! Stop the car! We are getting out!'*

*Reaching the edge of Far Flung, the car hasn't rightly come to a halt, when that same mass of old timers, still piteously screaming, but also clawing, punching and biting now, tumble thankfully onto the road, the old bagpiper landing on top of the heap. As chance would have it, the bagpiper's head lands much nearer the ground than does his feet, the result being that his kilt hangs down towards the former when it should be hanging down towards the latter, silvery moonlight, meantime, shining brightly on irrefutable evidence that the old fellow is very much a 'true' Scotsman.*

*Adding to the drama, in the melee of exiting the car, somebody has unceremoniously trampled on the abandoned bagpipes, expelling what little air is left in the bag.*

*And on that note, what had, for some, turned out to be a 'journey of sheer terror', concludes with what sounds suspiciously like a derisive rasping fart.*

Starting the unmarked car, and pulling away from the cemetery gates, Willie experiences a tremor of belated shame pass through him at the memory.

Yes, in the fifties, he is totally out of control - at his wildest - his life at its most chaotic.

His eyes mist over.

The day's events and the flood of memories are making him physically and mentally weary, and the shake of his hands are increasing, his desire for alcohol becoming unbearable. Also, the internal stabs of pain have intensified and perspiration is dampening his brow.

Eager for the comfort of Finlay's company and a good slug of whisky, he pushes down on the accelerator of the unmarked car.

Iain Ferguson

## SEVEN

And so it is, that after a week and a half on Skye, Willie finds himself on the southbound evening train to Glasgow.

There has been another murder - killing no 7. The killer has returned, yet again, to Glasgow: Same pattern. Another Englishman. Another riddle. But where the first five riddles threaten *'more to come'* and riddle number 6 hints at *'nearly done'*, number 7 is now declaring, *'one to come.'* As Ewan MacLeod had said, it is to be hoped that an end to the madness is in sight.

On the train now, Willie's attention focuses on the riddles. So far, neither himself nor the others involved in the investigation have come up with anything conclusive as to their meaning, except for one ray of faint possibility in the overall fog of confusion. It was Sgt McRae had suggested it. It was riddle number 3 and the assumption that the killer was a Gael, had put the sergeant onto it.

*'Twice twenty plus five.'* That made 45. Could that be a reference to 1745, the year of the Jacobite rebellion, leading up to the battle of Culloden - a long time Gaelic grievance? Applying a Gaelic context to each riddle then, it might be logical to assume that they also refer to Gaelic grievances or injustices - real or perceived.

The train has been fifteen minutes under way and Willie has the customary large glass of whisky on the table before him, along with the seven murder riddles spread out in the order of their occurrence. Bracketed after each riddle is the now guessed at 'Gaelic' solution.

No 1. Useful for sleep, but they made us weep

- more to come!

Signed L

*(Sheep - the 'Year of the Sheep', when Gaels were evicted from their land to make way for the lucrative wool yielding animals.)*

No 2. Not Black men, who then?

- more to come!

Signed O

*(White Settlers - the cultural destruction of Gaeldom by southern immigration.)*

No 3. Twice twenty plus five, so few left alive.

- more to come!

Signed C

*(1745. The Jacobite rebellion, leading to the Battle of Culloden and the end of the old clan system.)*

No 4. To increase the heat, will they need the peat?

- more to come!

Signed K

*(The 'Year of The Burnings' when Gaels' homes were put to the torch in the furtherance of eviction.)*

No 5. They'll sever your tongue, then you are done

- more to come!

Signed T

*(The officially sanctioned UK policy, up until the First World War, aimed at destroying the Gaelic language.)*

No 6. Follows the first, but by far it's the worst!

- almost done!

Signed I

*(The Highland Clearances, the official policy of eviction and 'encouraged' emigration.)*

No 7. We will sleep well when the Butcher's in Hell!

- one to come!

Signed T

*(The Duke of Cumberland - The Bloody Butcher - England's most bloodthirsty and obscene destroyer of the Scottish Gael.)*

Willie shuffles the papers on the carriage table before him. Yes, he and his colleagues on Skye have concluded that the killer is more than likely a Gael, some demented soul with a pathological grudge against what is termed White Settlers. They also reckon, in broad terms, that they have established the meaning and purpose of the riddles.

But what about the letters of signature? And what about the apparently pre-planned number of murders? The letters of signature include two Ts. It is logical to assume that it all adds up to some intentional pattern - some message. Is it in the letters of signature then, lies the vital clue to the killer's identity?

Willie continues to juggle the letters, frowning in concentration at the results:

LOCKTIT. LICKTOT. KILCOTT.

They don't make sense.

He sips at his whisky and in an increasing alcoholic haze peers through the condensation filmed glass at the yellow window reflections, undulating on the banked snow by the side of the track, his thoughts wandering.

- *Every man has his prejudices* -

Alex Craig's declaration comes to him through the night, triggering a rush of disjointed shadowy episodes from the past threads of his life, flashing now across his thoughts, bursting forth, one after another; episodes which had previously been confined to the subconscious - perhaps because the reality of them had been too 'inconvenient' or 'uncomfortable' to acknowledge. Now, for some obscure reason, his drifting thoughts are seeking these episodes out, dusting them down at last for apprehensive and long overdue scrutiny. . .

. . . and in the rippling banks of passing night snow, the images of

Rachel and Effie emerge. Rachel and Effie McQueen, two maiden grand aunts, both now dead; stay-at-home spinsters who, in the absence of available partners, and in assisting their older late sister Polly, had sacrificed their lives to caring for the *Bodach* and *Cailleach* - their ageing parents: Rachel and Effie, who had adored children, who had doted on Willie's own vacationing child Angus, endlessly baby-sitting him, clutching him to withered unfulfilled breasts. Rachel and Effie - always there, ever dependable, taken for granted by one and all; ever smiling across unnoticed sadness, and longing for what might have been.

Oh, certainly, he had recognised the tragedy that had been his grand aunts' lives, but he hadn't paid too much attention; had in fact exploited the convenience of them in his own mad breathless scramble to clutch at life. And now he is seeing these thankless lives again, but with the fine clarity of distance and time - in memory - when it is all too late to make amends.

And he had wondered about his prejudices!

Oh yes, Alex Craig, Willie Morrison has his prejudices sure enough: Willie Morrison is prejudiced in favour of himself - incorrigibly in favour of Willie Morrison!

And as the train groans south, Willie Morrison's newly acknowledged, seemingly endless prejudices are spewing like vomit from the depths of Willie Morrison's soul - guilty revelations from which it seems his thoughts are now unable to escape; and he remembers Donnie's death in Glasgow, his younger brother Donnie, the talented one of the family - an artist, a poet, had he bothered to try: A premature death - another wasted life!

*'We are afraid it's bad news, Mr Morrison,'* had been the hospital phone message. With mother by now dead and the siblings scattered around the world, Willie is the nearest next of kin. The hospital message continues: *'Your brother Donald is rather poorly. We would suggest that you come as soon as possible.'*

On his way to the hospital, he succumbs, predictably, to his weakness, his cowardice, skulking into a city bar for liquid courage, gulping several large whiskies, one on the tail of the other, and where he copiously weeps, alone in a corner - desolate rasping sobs. And then the sobs abruptly stop, and he will never weep for Donnie again. A light though has gone out in his life, not totally extinguished but locked in a treasured memory store, deep within him.

'Look, Willie!' Donnie had croaked from the hospital bed. 'Look!' He is gazing at the ward ceiling and Willie follows the gaze but sees only the ward ceiling.

'What is it Donnie?'

'Clouds, Willie! Look! Clouds!. Beautiful clouds! . . . I'm going on a journey Willie.' And it is confirmed to him at that moment; Donnie believes in God - is referring to Heaven.

God!

The snowbanks, meantime, are a rushing blur beyond the carriage window.

God! Ah yes, Ewan MacLeod's God. The same God of whom he himself has been so smugly dismissive, but from whom Donnie was, at that moment in hospital, receiving grace and serenity, so evident in the radiance of his prematurely dying poet's face. And, oh, he had needed that serenity, that final strength, because Willie, spewing the fumes of his weakness, had been incapable of providing it - to the brother he had professed to love, the youngest and gentlest of the siblings, whose touch and scent, whose brotherly bond had given of his own reassurance and strength in that childhood attic bedroom of dark and stormy Hebridean nights. And he had let him down, had failed to return that strength, that bond of reassurance, when his brother had needed it most - in the final lonely hour! And because he had been inarticulate and incapable, having indulged his own needs first, his cowardice, in a sleazy city bar. And wasn't that, now, the ultimate prejudice - a prejudice in favour of self?

He tightens his grip on the whisky glass.

At that moment in the hospital, he had had the chance to gather his brother up in his arms, cradle his head to his chest, and tell him how very much he loved him - how much they all loved him - but he hadn't and his very last chance had gone as his beloved brother passed away.

And whereas Old Maggie had been buried beside family and ancestors, in the wind lulled peace of a Hebridean shore, Donnie, because it had been 'convenient', in truth, hadn't been taken 'home' to Skye, as had been his final whispered request, but buried in a vandalised city cemetery. Whereas Old Maggie lay within earshot of black faced sheep and mountain stream and screaming hawk, Donnie's grave was spread with city grime and ruffled by the endless snarl of indifferent passing traffic - indifferent passing strangers. And all because it had been 'convenient'!

Oh yes, Alex Craig, you were right about prejudices, dead right, and more honest than Willie Morrison.

He sips absently at yet another whisky and lights yet another cigarette. The eating beast is particularly bad this evening. He shuffles the signatures on the table again and gets TICKLOT - yet more apparent nonsense.

He is aware of Skye slipping further and further into the darkness behind him, aware that he had, in truth, returned to it as a stranger; and he remembers his recently increasing lament about these other 'strangers' - the White Settlers - who were swamping it. Well, why shouldn't they? Had that lament too not illustrated prejudice? Why shouldn't strangers fill the space he himself had vacated? Why hadn't he stayed and fought it, had he felt that strongly? What did he want? A land that was empty and silent - a museum to Willie Morrison's sentimentality, Willie Morrison's nostalgia?

And of the Gaels who had remained behind, what did he want of them? To remain museum pieces? And again to justify Willie Morrison's sentimentality? Wasn't it only clawing nostalgia now, tied Willie Morrison to his Gaelic past? The land of his origins had changed and, having deserted it, he himself had changed with it, but in a different direction. Only in his memory did it stand as it had once stood, and the realisation of that change had confused and annoyed him.

He had called on relations and old friends during his visit. Initially, the meetings had been enthusiastic. Old stories and old escapades had been brought out and examined, but his attention had wandered and he had known that the attentions of his friends had wandered also. In reality, he had returned as but a ghost, an uncomfortable reminder. Gaeldom had slipped on and had changed and all of them with it. Returning, he realised that he had been as changed to them as they to him. When he had left so long before he had effectively died and so had become fixed and unchangeable. His return had caused only confusion and uneasiness - had muddied the waters. Although they would never say it of course, he sensed that they had gradually wanted him gone again, wanted him to resume his place in the pattern of remembrance.

He sips at the whisky and thinks about Sarah.

Sarah herself wasn't Highland, was 'Central Belt'; she didn't particularly like the Highlands, felt no great affinity with the Gaelic race. He knew that much of that was of his own doing, because all things Gaelic he had made competitors for his affections, had placed them in a prominent position in his thoughts, and had resented Sarah's apparent indifference to them.

'You live in the past, Willie', Sarah had said, 'In an apathetic make believe world of sentimental Gaelic past. You have Angus and I now, your main responsibility. Life is *now* Willie. Face up to that fact. If you don't you will destroy us - your own family! I can't - won't - let that happen. I keep telling you this. You hear but you don't listen, you just don't *listen* Willie. Angus and I have our dreams too. Dreams that lie beyond sentimental Gaeldom. I believe you love us in your own way, hopefully love us dearly as we love you, but it isn't quite enough Willie, if you are too wrapped up in that nostalgic dream world of yours to listen.'

He drains the whisky in his glass.

Dream world! Dear Lord, how right Sarah had been. Dream world. Perhaps there lay the answer he had so long sought to grasp, when considering his confusion of emotions with regards to Skye. Perhaps it wasn't to do with the invasion by strangers at all, but with an inner wasteland of nostalgia and over sentimentalised memory - with unreality.

He has a sudden passing thought about the killer he is presently hunting down. If the latter is indeed a Gael, is he drawing pointless, deadly motivation from that same sentimentalized wasteland?

He shuffles the signature on the table. TOCKLIT. He pours a flood of whisky into his empty glass and gulps a large gulp.

- *You just don't listen, Willie -*

He glances through the carriage window at the rippling passing snow, banked high by the side of the track, and gasps with disbelief. Pressing his face against the cold glass and peering intently he can see, in the ripples, the image of Angus - Angus as an eager plump faced toddler, racing bright eyed towards him, little arms outstretched, his lips forming words that can't be heard within the carriage. But Willie knows what the words are saying - knows exactly! He has heard them so many times before:

'LIFT ME, DADDY! - LIFT ME, DADDY! - LIFT ME, DADDY!

Laying the whisky glass on the table, he half rises and places both hands on the window, his face pressing harder against it, eyes wide, his breath coming in short sharp gasps. Angus is running as fast as his little child legs will allow, arms outstretched, periodically tumbling into the snow drifts and desperately rising again, continuing to run but inevitably losing ground, his image sliding back towards the rear of the moving train, the silent words spilling from his mouth.

LIFT ME, DADDY!

Pressing his face even closer to the glass, Willie tries to squint sideways towards the vanishing image - and then it is gone beyond view. Breathing heavily, he falls back into his seat and leans his head against the headrest, his eyes tight shut.

Hallucinating now! What next - delirium tremens?! For God's sake, man, pull yourself together! Sober up! Please - sober up!

Of all the ghosts in his life, of all the skeletons in his cupboard, along with Sarah of course, Angus is the one that subconsciously haunts and troubles him most. Hands shaking, he reaches for the whisky glass. Unbelievably, it is already empty. Fumbling for the half bottle he pours its dregs into the glass. It is the second half bottle he has consumed since bidding Finlay farewell at the crossroads to board the morning bus. And the train rolls interminably south. Another twenty minutes and they will be arriving at Fort William.

His fingers absently juggle the signatures. They say COLKITT. He moves the K then quickly brings it back. Despite the alcoholic haze, he tenses with rising interest.

COLKITT!?

COLKITT !! Yes, by God, that could be it!

He checks the column of names on sergeant McRae's preliminary list of transient travellers from Glasgow to Skye and vice versa. Two of those listed bear a certain name - a name that now interests him!

The train is scheduled for the customary quarter hour stop at Fort William Station in order to attach an engine to the rear carriage which, in the dead end track, has now become the lead carriage.

Willie takes the opportunity to phone Ewan MacLeod from the station bar and gets him in.

'Ewan? Willie here. I'm at Fort William station and I haven't got long. Have there been any more? . . . More killings?'

'I'm afraid so, Willie. This very afternoon. In Glasgow again. Same old pattern. Same old everything. But there is some definite hope in this one. He just might be keeping his promise, because the riddle ends with, *now it is done!* We are all praying that……'

'Ewan! The signature, Ewan! It is O, is it not? . . . Ewan!'

Ewan hears the sharp expectant breathing at the other end of the line.

'Yes Willie. It is indeed O. How the devil….?'

'There is a strong possibility that the killer is an Alistair McDonald, Ewan.'

'Good Heavens, you're not onto him Willie? My God, how…?'

'No Ewan, I'm not onto him at all. I don't know him from Adam. All I'm saying is that someone called Alistair McDonald could be our man. I have details in my possession of two of that name with whom we can begin. Listen, the guard is blowing his whistle Ewan. The train is about to leave, I'll have to go.' He hangs up.

The train has started to move by the time he reaches the platform and he is required to sprint to catch it. He is gasping for breath as he sits down. It takes him several minutes to recover. He is feeling decidedly unwell. Health-wise, it has been another very bad day. He lights a cigarette and opens the half whisky bottle he had bought at the station bar. He adds an O to the letters on the table.

COLKITTO !

Yes! COLKITTO! He feels very hopeful that before him now lies the solution to the letters of signature, but he isn't experiencing the enthusiasm or elation he normally would have.

Jesus! The eating beast was wicked tonight.

The three fellow passengers of earlier have disembarked at Fort William and he has the carriage to himself. He slurps at the whisky and gazes at his reflection in the carriage window.

 - *You just don't listen, Willie* -

 - *Lift me, daddy!* - *Lift me, daddy!*

He leans against the head rest and closes his eyes...

   ... and time passes . . .

When he opens his eyes again, he glances at his watch, surprised that exactly one hour has slipped by since leaving Fort William and that the train is now rattling across the savage and desolate Rannoch Moor. He peers out at its bleak moon silvered emptiness. This is where he had recently come in, but he is travelling south now. It seems such an alien direction in which to be travelling, as if his soul is inexorably emptying.

Jesus - the eating beast!

The sprint for the train hasn't helped. A tight constriction sears his insides and he places his forehead against the cool of the carriage window. A herd of deer beside a lone wind-blasted tree is faintly visible, dark shadows on the moonlit snow - alert and wary, resentful of the clanking intrusion of man and his infernal machines.

He downs a particularly large swallow of whisky, so large that it seems to scald his senses, and he finds himself panting slightly. For a moment the scene outside turns hazy and he closes his eyes again, remaining motionless, embers of warmth beginning to glow within him . . .

   . . . it is more a faint disturbance of air, rather than any sound, makes him aware of a sudden presence and he opens his eyes and sees the stranger moving down the central corridor towards him. He hadn't been aware of the train stopping at the remote moorland station, nor had he heard anyone come through what are noisy connecting carriage doors, and this strikes him as odd. The stranger is a tall man, gaunt and very thin, spectral, dressed entirely in black; black frock-coated suit, black shoes, black shirt, black string tie. Even his flat crowned, wide brimmed hat is black. As he walks he expertly shuffles a pack of cards in his hands.

Uneasy, Willie tenses.

As the stranger comes closer his eyes become evident beneath the brim of the hat; peculiar blue eyes, the blue being so pale they are barely distinguishable from the white of the eyeballs. This makes the pinpoint black of the pupils stand out - piercing and rather menacing. The skin of the face is also very pale and parchment-like and stretched taut across unusually high cheek bones. Coming to a halt on reaching Willie, the stranger looks down towards him, a thin mouth showing the trace of a bizarre frosty smile that doesn't look right, the hands, meantime, still shuffling the pack of cards. He speaks:

'Good evening, Pilgrim.' There is a breathless softness in his voice.

'Eh... good evening yourself, stranger.'

'I don't suppose you will mind me joining you Pilgrim,' continues the stranger, sitting down uninvited across the carriage table from Willie.

'Eh... I suppose not,' replies Willie, vaguely annoyed. 'Are you a gambler, stranger?'

'Ah, - the cards!'

The stranger's hypnotic eyes flick quickly up to survey him momentarily before flicking down to the cards again, cards which he is now mixing, fanning, boxing and spinning around his fingers with great dexterity. 'They aren't playing cards, Pilgrim'

'What kind of cards are they then?'

'They are the cards of life, Pilgrim - the cards of destiny. Everybody's life and destiny are recorded in these cards.'

'Everybody?'

'That's correct Pilgrim. I have a duty, when the time comes, to go over everybody's life with them and discuss their destiny.' The stranger's eyes flick up briefly again, the cards in his hands by now a blur of complex motion. 'There comes a time when most people require to be reminded of the myriad episodes of their lives, and the consequences of these episodes; how it all impacts on their destiny. Others, a minority, already know themselves and can tell me.'

The thin smile, that doesn't look right, widens a fraction.

'I sense that you, Pilgrim, are one of the latter, that you can tell me. Would I be right?'

Willie's eyes narrow. 'Normally, I would consider that my life is nobody's business but mine, and your presumption rather impertinent stranger. But oddly enough, for some reason, I am feeling inclined to indeed tell you. So for that reason I will.'

The stranger's attention returns to the cards, his small piercing pupils gazing at the whirling designs and manoeuvres he is performing now on the tabletop.

Eventually, Willie continues.

'I am a strange man. An odd complex man, in actual fact. Indeed, a flawed and disturbed man might be more accurate - I have to concede that myself. To understand life, the way a man turns out, whether, broadly, he is good or bad, I believe that one must go back and start at the beginning, to what happens in childhood. There are those who would disagree with that theory, who maintain that while a person is born innocent and intrinsically good, and can make a conscious decision or effort to maintain that goodness, he can also make a calculated decision to indulge in evil, if it is to his or her advantage. I have a friend who believes the latter and maintains that using traumatic incidents in childhood to excuse wayward behaviour in later life is so much mumbo jumbo - convenient excuses.'

The stranger continues to gaze at the whirling cards on the table.

'That will be Ewan? Ewan MacLeod?'

'That's right! How the . . .?'

'The cards, Pilgrim. As I said, everybody is in the cards.'

Willie reaches for his whisky glass.

'I wouldn't touch that stuff, Pilgrim.' The stranger doesn't look up. 'Poison! It's merely a prop. A crutch. You don't really need it.'

Willie's trembling hand coils around the glass but he doesn't raise it.

'It all began for me, I suppose, with my very earliest memory of rejection - or what I fancied to be rejection. It was a little white dog. I was only three years old but I still remember it, as if it was only yesterday, and I still remember the little dog's name - *Sporran*. On coming through to my parents' bedroom, as I often did of a morning before they were awake, I would see Sporran lying smugly on top of the bed between them, lying where my childhood instincts reckoned that that's where I should be. That always hurt and angered me. Subsequently, away from prying eyes, poor Sporran was to suffer dearly and regularly for his innocent treachery.'

Willie pauses.

'This all took place in the city of Glasgow. My parents, Skye born and bred, moved there looking for work before I was born, which was between the Great Wars. Anyway, continuing the rejection theme, the Second World War came along and myself and two brothers, being young children, were evacuated for safety's sake to Skye for the war's duration, to be cared for by our maternal grandparents. The distances involved and the cost and difficulty of travel in those days had dictated that we didn't really know our grandparents that well. While my younger brother reveled in the evacuation my older brother detested it. I reveled in it too, as it subsequently turned out. But, at the beginning, to me there was a hint of parental betrayal in it - another imagined rejection. The long and short of it was, our grandparents turned out to be kindly wonderful guardians, whom we grew to adore. But then . . . '

Willie makes to raise the whisky glass but stops himself.

' . . . but then, five years down the road - war over! I was now required to leave people and a place I had grown to love and didn't want to leave, in order to return to Glasgow. Imagined betrayal yet again! Imagined rejection yet again! Next blow was the death of my father, leaving the hard work of bringing up a young family in a violent city to our widowed mother. By this time I belonged to, or was of, two different places - Glasgow and Skye, and of two different cultures - English-speaking Lowland Scottish, and Gaelic speaking Highland. Then again, depending on how you looked at it, I belonged to neither - I was in a no man's land in between. To my way of thinking, *belonging* has to be 100%. Less than that is not *belonging* at all. Had I written my life story at that time, I could have titled it *Adrift in a Gael,* because I felt myself to be just that - adrift - a lost soul, belonging to nowhere and to no one. So, the rejection theme continues!'

There is a momentary silence.

'My preference however was always the Highland one and, like my younger brother Donnie, it was always as a Gael that I presented myself and intuitively considered myself to be. It was more mystical and poetical, you see, more romantic and dramatic - the fearless Celtic warrior, the noble savage and all that malarkey. That said, I had never been long enough in Gaeldom to become fully integrated into the Gaelic community. As a result, it seemed as if I was always to remain on the outside of where I considered my rightful place to be - underlining my general sense of rejection!'

Willie falls silent again, a longer silence. The stranger is still juggling the cards, but Willie is aware of the raised piercing eyes regarding him.

'You are doing well, Pilgrim. You are telling your story very well. Do continue.'

Willie sighs and continues. 'It was hard for my mother, old Flora, bringing up children alone in a dangerous city on a measly widow's pension. She did well though, taking on part-time work; educating us, dressing us respectably, feeding us healthily, teaching us manners and the importance of honest endeavour and Christian moral standards. But that said, I also had my disappointments in her. By that I mean that she was too inhibited to show her emotions to her children, to tell them how much she loved them, how well they were doing. I had so often yearned for her arm around my shoulder, reassuring, pulling me close, a warm whisper expressing love of me. It wasn't Flora's fault, of course. Being a widow alone, she had her worries about us. She was working hard, had bills to pay, physical exhaustion. There wouldn't really be time for the luxury of emotion, I suppose.'

Following another silence, a tightness comes into Willie's voice, the stranger still studying him.

'And then the bloody roof fell in! My world falls apart! Enter the *family friend!* This *friend*, Albert by name, takes me in hand - a vulnerable lad of eleven or twelve. He promises me the moon. He undertakes to indulge my passion and buy me a motorcycle when I will be old enough. He will teach me to drive cars. Meantime, he takes me on fishing trips. Takes me camping. He takes me on foreign holidays. He has the money. Flora is happy. At least one of her boys is being looked after, is having a good time. It is less for her to worry about. But of all of Flora's boys, why has he picked on me? I have Alpha leanings. In my boyish imagination I am Tarzan, I am a fighter pilot, I am a gunfighter of the Old West, I am a bull fighter - I am whatever macho all-action hero I have last seen at the cinema, or have last read about in the latest novel, which makes what Albert has got planned for me all the more humiliating and destructive.'

Hearing the break in Willie's voice, the stranger continues to study him. 'You are doing well Pilgrim, very well. Don't stop now. Get it all out, out of your system. You have to understand your life and why you are who you are. I already know what Albert did, but it has to come from your own lips.'

'If you already know, goddammit, I can't understand why I have to repeat it.'

Willie fights an urge to raise the whisky glass to his mouth. It is an effort having to say what he has to say and there is another brief pause.

'The bastard sexually abused me - *sexually abused me*!!! Every night, when camping or in hotel rooms, my ordeal begins with his inappropriate intimate touching and caressing - his disgusting pawing and physical intrusions. And when he is finished with me, satiated and untroubled, and having stolen yet more of my innocence . . . my happiness . . . my life . . . he falls contentedly asleep. I don't sleep though - can't sleep! Unbroken peaceful sleep is the preserve of the un-hunted. Distraught and revolted and diminished, I will spend the remainder of the night, like other pursued creatures of the darkness, silently screaming, until dawn temporarily releases me' A pained whimper rises from Willie's throat. 'Just the memory of it! The memory of what the bastard did! I can't go on! I can't go on!'

'Take your time Pilgrim, take your time. You are doing well. A deep breath and carry on.'

'Well, during this terrible time, I am leading a double life, am being forced to live in yet another two different worlds. There is the macho, dramatic all-action hero-world I long to inhabit and present to others. And there is the dark secretive Albert-world of paedophilic sexual depravity and mental torment, which I am desperate to escape and conceal. As a result, I am in turmoil, I become withdrawn; I have no sense of self-worth and I lose my confidence; I am, incredibly, filled with guilt. When I reach the legal age, this gravitates to the consumption of alcohol, which I discover banishes shyness and inhibition and allows me to present the image of manliness I am so desperate to present . . .'

'You are doing well, Pilgrim. Keep going. Get it all out.'

'. . . Increasingly, a byproduct of all this turmoil is anger - black rages - fist fights in city bars and back streets. But much of that is merely image. And reinforcing the image, are my props. I grow my hair wild and long. I sport a drooping Zapata moustache. You have to remember that this is the mid-fifties - years before such imagery will became somewhat commonplace. Conscription to the armed forces is still in force - a fate I avoid, on account of my becoming an Art student. Short back and sides are the accepted, respectable norm. Long haired, unkempt louts are a disgrace, a threat to society. Years later, people will tell me how *terrified* they had been of the drunken *wild man* I had been in those days. These belated revelations shock and shame me: other than fisticuffs, it has never been in me to physically hurt anyone. Head butting, kicking or offensive weapons are anathema to my nature. It is all about image and prop - mirrors and smoke - bluff! And it is a bluff that is very effective, since adversaries invariably back down. But even this isn't enough during these confused times. I have to be wilder and even more dramatic still and this leads me into the dangerous world of motorcycle racing.'

He pauses, his thoughts lingering in some past place.

'You may ask, why I didn't just walk away from this Albert pervert. Well, I felt trapped. Who did I tell? How could I explain? Would anybody believe me? Incredible as it may seem, I felt deep shame - as if everything must be my fault! And then again, in the earlier years of this tormented liaison, for a young lad from an impoverished family, the prospect of motorcycles, driving cars, fishing trips and exotic holidays is just too good to be true. Of course, the price that has to be paid - sexual abuse - is way too much. But then again, I always have the hope, and genuinely believe, that the abuse simply can't last. Very soon, I reason, somebody must surely realise what is going on and come to my aid. They don't of course. And hatred of Albert builds up within me. Submissive compliance and revulsion become, increasingly, indignation and outrage. But, as I said, who do I tell, and will they believe me? As my anger and resentment grow, Albert realises it, but his depraved addiction is too strong for him to resist. Then it happens! Unable to take any more, I break and fly into a rage that surprises even myself.'

Willie pauses again, frowning at the memory.

'I can still see the terrified Albert, cowering naked in a corner of the room as I stand over him, my fists clenched. He begins to cry, pleading that I don't tell a soul about our relationship. In those days, homosexuality is still against the law. The strange thing is, I unbelievably feel suddenly sorry for Albert. He had been grooming me, of course, and he was a past master at the grooming, but in the process, in many ways he had been generous and deviously good to me, professed to be genuinely fond of me. Even years later, during rare chance meetings, I will acknowledge him and exchange a few words. And I never did tell. Possibly, he too had had his childhood traumas, making him the way he was. Who knows? He is long dead now, but the apocalyptic fallout from his abuse lived on. The damage had been done. My life was a mess, will remain flawed and ruined. I continue, even to this day, to be unsure of myself, and my answer is still subconscious anger and the bottle.'

Impulsively, Willie throws the whisky glass to his lips and drains it. He turns then and smiles wanly at the stranger, who remains silent, sadly shaking his head.

'You only think that I don't need a drink stranger. But I do - believe me!' There is another pause. ' Anyway, back to the happy story . . . Worst of all, what should have been my normal sex life is at times to be adversely effected. Despite everything, I was, and still am a highly sexed heterosexual male with a great love of and desire for women. And I had more than my fair share of intimate affairs in my day, I reckon, but at times the fallout from the Albert years could be an issue. To become intimately close to a woman, I often required the Dutch courage of alcohol. And sometimes, in the process of being intimate, out of nowhere, the image of Albert and his depraved activities with me- my *shameful secret* - would fill my head. At such times my performance would invariably fall away, making me effectively impotent. With short term liaisons there usually were no issues. The real problems arose when there was the possibility of long-term commitment. With commitment comes closeness, and with closeness comes trust and the possibility of falling in love. And with trust and falling in love comes the danger of being rejected - of being hurt. That was the logic of my sub conscious mind - crazy, crazy logic!'

Rubbing his brow in agitation, Willie pauses a moment.

The ironic thing is, stranger, as a young boy, before Albert came along, I had so often fantasised about how my first romantic experience would be. I had it all mapped out. I had seen it often after all, in the movies. It would be Hollywood stuff ..Walt Disney! . . . buttercup meadows . . . babbling brooks . . . soft mountain breezes . . cotton wool clouds . . . cooing doves. *My girl* and I would fling us down in waving meadow grass and embrace - an embrace the likes of which the world had never witnessed.'

Pausing again, he glances across at the stranger and utters a hollow laugh.

'But it wasn't to be anything remotely like that at all - was it stranger? Albert had seen to that! And you know something else, stranger? Even at that young age, hopeless romantic and fantasist that I then was, I knew who *my girl* just has to be. Only she would do!'

He repeats the hollow laugh. 'And I know what you are now going tell me: you have never heard such a load of bullshit! Syrupy sentimental bullshit - Right?'

The stranger glances up and their eyes lock. He smiles his bizarre frosty smile, that doesn't look right. 'No Pilgrim, I won't tell you that at all. I have listened to a great deal of sentimental bullshit over the years. Some of it mushier and even more syrupy than yours. But what I will tell you is the name of your just-had-to-be *girl* . . . Rosie-Anne - Right?'

Unblinking, their eyes remain locked.

'And that will be the cards tell you that, stranger. Everybody is in the cards - right? These damned cards are something else!'

Willie's eyes fall away and land on the empty whisky glass.

'There are so many confusions, so many forgotten incidents tumbling around in my subconscious right now. Even as I speak, yet another set of incidents I had forgotten about come to mind. As I told you, I was evacuated during the war to my grandparents' care in Skye. Periodically, during that time, we are inflicted by visits from a neurotic grand aunt - grand aunt Polly! When I say inflicted, I mean *inflicted!* Grand aunt Polly was a spinster, in her late thirties at the time and hysterical that she is being, *left on the shelf.* Wildly over-sexed and with hormones permanently running amok, Polly is constantly screaming with fright. Drop a plate or bang a drawer or loudly shut a door and Polly will utter a piercing scream of fright. She is a neurotic and fading Southern Belle - straight out of a Tennessee Williams play. She is Blanche du Bois from A Streetcar Named Desire. Her most damaging foibles, from my point of view however, are her periodic lungings at my, a young boy's, groin. She will then raise her hand aloft in triumph while displaying her thumb, which is trapped and peering helplessly from between her first and second fingers. *Look!* She will trumpet. *Look! I've caught your wee man! I've caught your wee man!* She obviously has a penis fixation'

Willie's frown deepens at the memory.

'In humouring Polly, other women present, not really meaning to be unkind, laugh at the *joke*. I of course feel outraged and humiliated - diminished. Just another ingredient to add to the whole sorry story, I suppose'

While remaining engrossed in the spinning cards, the stranger speaks:

'You described these events as, *forgotten episodes*, but you hadn't forgotten them at all, Pilgrim. You remembered them just there. You wanted to forget them, but you have remembered them many times without you knowing it. The memories were there at the back of your mind all the time. Deep rooted - all these years. Psychologically, your subconscious is quite a mess Pilgrim. And most of the mess is sexual. Complicating the issue is the fact that your memories of actual or imagined betrayal . . . rejection . . . humiliation . . . invariably place the blame on those you loved or trusted.'

Willie's laugh is again hollow:

'But doesn't psychiatry tell us that everything has to do with sex, stranger? Psychiatrists maintain that the world is motivated and fashioned by sex - couldn't exist without it; that it is sex makes the world go round. But then again, psychiatrists are a strange and wacky bunch – even nuttier than the rest of us.'

Willie makes to lift the whisky glass again, forgetting it is empty.

'I have to admit stranger, that all in all, my life hasn't really been a happy or successful one. Oh yes, there were happy moments, very happy moments, but they were transient; beyond them there were always clouds on the horizon. Deep down, I was always waiting for something bad to happen, waiting to be hurt, to be let down, usually, as you say, by those I loved and trusted. And increasingly, as time went on I would retaliate; I would hurt, and *test* the ones I loved and trusted first - a pre-emptive strike. As I grow older I am learning more and more about who I am; understanding more and more what made me how I am. My psychology is deeply flawed. The workings of my sub-conscious mind are cross wired. Oh yes, I am now aware of all that. And I am increasingly recognising that the main flaw of my life, my biggest sin, has been my general treatment of those I loved, especially my beautiful wife Sarah and my precious son Angus.'

Willie's voice threatens breakdown. Continuing to manipulate his cards, the stranger doesn't look up. .

'Keep going. Keep going, Pilgrim. As the old adage says: *you always hurt the ones you love, the ones you shouldn't hurt at all.* That's what you're saying, Pilgrim. I hear that lament all the time, I'm afraid.'

Willie continues:

'This periodic testing/hurting thing, this pre-emptive strike business, was so very dreadful, stranger. Some of the hurtful things I said, starting from away back, to my brothers and even to my poor mother, all of whom I adored, were quite unbelievable. But the words would spill forth spontaneously, like some form of Tourette's. And they were almost immediately and terribly regretted. But they, my loved ones, had been *tested,* had learned what it was like to be *hurt.* This behaviour seemed to appease my insecurity, like a drug - but only until the next time! What twisted goddamned behaviour!'

He pauses, toying with his empty glass

'By the time poor Sarah comes along, this *testing* and *hurting* thing has become a deadly paranoia. Let me tell you about Sarah, stranger. She is so beautiful. Her huge honey brown eyes are so open and honest. When she smiles the cheeks of her broad face are deeply dimpled. Her physical beauty is echoed by the beauty of her soul. She is possessed of no avarice or envy. She covets nobody or nothing. She sees the good in everyone. Sounds too good to be true, but true it is. But she was blind - must have been - to fall for and marry the damaged goods, the heavy drinking waster and fantasist that was me. I was Dr Jekyll and Mr Hyde. She had been introduced to and fell for Jekyll. She was yet to meet Hyde!'

His eyes drift far away through the carriage window.

'But I did make an effort to build a solid future for us. Before Sarah I had aspirations of becoming an artist. I'm not sure how deep my artistic talents went. I won entry to the Glasgow School of Art, but too much drinking and brawling and I was expelled, so I never found out. Being the person I am, perhaps it was the *drama* of being an artist - the suffering undiscovered creative genius in his freezing attic - more than any real talent, that drove me in that direction. However, with the arrival of Sarah I pulled myself together and, using my Gaelic contacts, I was accepted into the Glasgow police force.'

The stranger's piercing pupils remain intent upon the intricacy of the latest card formation unfolding on the table.

'Using your *Gaelic contacts*? Alex Craig would have something to say about that one, Pilgrim.'

Willie grunts ironically. 'Ah, yes - Alex Craig. *One in, all in together boys.* You were right yet again Alex . . . but getting back to Sarah, the testing/hurting thing is becoming more frequent. Deep down, I can't accept that someone like Sarah can see anything in me. There has to be a catch, which I have to pre-empt. The tests/hurts become more frequent, and not quite so spontaneous but calculated, which makes them even more inexcusable. Then comes the test/hurt that is tantamount to outright betrayal - inexcusable betrayal. In a Glasgow street one day, Fate decrees that I bump into a woman I had fallen for many years before but, on account of my chaotic behaviour and lack of confidence, I had lost her to another man. The marriage hadn't lasted and she is now divorced. We begin an affair - an affair that is destined, frankly, to subsequently destroy my life.'

Willie is by now absently spinning his empty whisky glass on the tabletop.

'Sarah finds out about the affair. But then she is supposed to find out. I make sure that she does. It is a *test*, a *hurting*, goddammit! She has to join the club of the betrayed and rejected. Or that's what my twisted subconscious is telling me. On the other hand, when the dust has settled, all will be fine. I will apologise, as always. I will be consumed by genuine regret - I will atone. I consider myself to be of little worth, so my actions are of no great consequence. Simple as that! We will understand each other. We will be strengthened by it. We will be a brotherhood, a brotherhood of the betrayed and rejected.' He sighs, long and deep before continuing. 'But this betrayal has been a miscalculation, a step too far - the cheating, the breaking of sacred and loving marriage vows! How can a man atone for *that*! How can a man ever make amends, or hope to be forgiven?'

The glass slips from Willie's hand and continues spinning on its own.

'Poor Sarah! The one I had loved the most in my life, has to endure the maelstrom of my flawed make-up, the full gamut! And not only is there the madness of the testing, of the hurting, but also there are my sexual hang-ups to endure - the *Albert effect* filling my head! So, at times, there can be issues – disinterest, impotency – and such issues, with the one you love, are an insult, an insensitivity, an outrage.'

His voice breaking, Willie pauses to catch his breath.

'At the end of the day, the terrible truth is that, added to everything else, Sarah isn't being physically fulfilled, as a woman in her prime should be. Oh God, that poor beautiful wonderful woman. And yet, despite her terrible hurt and betrayal, she *wants* to forgive me – tries to forgive me. As I said, her soul is open and large. There is nothing vindictive, spiteful or mean in her being. Despite all her efforts though, the burden of forgetting and forgiving my betrayal is too great. Despite her efforts, that particular betrayal - the hurt and ramifications of it - are always there, in the shadows between us, lying deep in the sadness of her beautiful eyes. Everybody loved Sarah. But she too loses her confidence, having to put on this brave face. To all outward appearances, she has a good and kind man, a presentable husband, the perfect marriage. We appear the perfect couple. But, in reality, being a betrayed and an unfulfilled woman, the strain of living a lie is all too much. She begins to drink heavily and to smoke too much. Eventually, she can't take any more and one day, smiling sadly and softly bidding me goodbye, she wishes me luck and walks away.'

Willie pauses to catch his breath again. 'After the crime, stranger, there has to be the punishment.'

Fighting the break in his voice, he reaches for the whisky bottle and replenishes his glass, filling it to the brim, but he doesn't raise it to his lips. 'And she takes our son with her of course - our son, our precious son.'

'Ah yes Pilgrim, your son. That will be Angus. Let's talk about Angus.'

The stranger's dancing hands slow down. Boxing the cards into a neat pile on the tabletop, he pushes them aside, his unsettling piercing gaze now concentrating solely on Willie.

'Yes Pilgrim, let's talk about Angus.'

Glancing at the boxed cards, motionless now, Willie continues.

'Unbelievably, even Angus, a child, my own son, falls within the sphere of my paranoia. How else can you explain my treatment of him, of my own precious son? The number of times I would arrive home from work, tired, often having had too many whiskies on the way. And there he is, wee chubby Angus, running down the hall to greet me, eyes alight and his arms outstretched: *Lift me, daddy! Lift me, daddy!*

And my response, on too many occasions? *Och, daddy is tired, my wee lamb. Daddy will lift you later* . . . Oh, dear Jesus!'

Willie places his face in his hands. *'Lift me, daddy! Lift me, daddy!* Oh, the privilege of that request. And I rejected it so often. I treasured and adored that wee guy so deeply but, as with Sarah, I couldn't adequately express it. Why? Why? Had my little son to be tested and punished too? Had he to learn the meaning of rejection? Oh, sure, I complied with wee Angus's request many times, but not nearly close to every time the request had been made and that, surely, was nowhere near enough. And the requests, so often rejected, became less and less and eventually ceased.'

Willie's face remains buried in his hands, his voice muffled.

'The number of days - always a *tomorrow* - that I had earmarked for *beginning again*, for making a *fresh start* and becoming an exemplary husband and father . . . human being . . . but it never happened. The demon within me wouldn't allow it. But even back then, I was aware that there was something far wrong with me, but I didn't know what it was, didn't know that what I was, was angry! Angry about things I had locked away, by way of denial, deep within me - things that frightened me because they hurt me or because I didn't understand them. The understanding of them would come to me eventually, bit by bit, but that understanding would come too late. Poor Angus! That poor innocent wonderful wee fellow! Oh, dear Jesus! If I only had my time back again - to make amends - to begin afresh'

The stranger sits back in his seat, picks up the neatly boxed cards from the table and places them in his coat pocket. Removing a gold watch and chain from his waistcoat, he opens the casing and glances at the time.

'You would be surprised Pilgrim, how many times I have heard that last lament - *if only I had my time back again.* Oh yes Pilgrim, many, many times.'

Placing his cheek on the backrest of his seat, Willie's eyes swing towards the carriage window. Beyond the glass, the full moon is nudging a distant, snow-capped mountain ridge.

'It was so unjust stranger, so terribly unjust, what events in my childhood did to me; how they made me the man I turned out to be - flawed and disturbed - a Jekyll and Hyde. I honestly believe that at heart I am a decent man, am capable of true love and of loyalty. I'm sure I have in me compassion and tenderness. I believe I have an innate sense of humour, although that has, by now, become the humour of the clown - a humour that merely masks regrets and sadness. But whatever, the things that happened to me in childhood *did* mould and change me. Of that I feel certain. Children, of course, can be quite resilient and surprisingly strong. They can assess and re-adjust and compartmentalise, more than adults realise. Some traumatic childhood events, while having long term effects, can be handled and coped with. But others, such as sexual abuse, cannot. Sexual abuse of a child leads to the destruction of that child's soul. The ramifications are lifelong. There is no escape. Paedophiles are in effect murderers - they murder the soul! And as with all murderers they have to be stopped, have to be punished. Not punished with Ewan's Big Stick. I don't believe in Big Sticks because they solve nothing. Perhaps I don't know the answer. It will take a greater mind than mine to determine what form the punishment should be - but it has to be effective!'

There is a long pause.

'The unfunny and alarming thing is, stranger, I have at times briefly wondered, what if Ewan MacLeod is right. What if people like me do use unpleasant or traumatic events experienced in childhood to excuse or justify our unacceptable behaviour in later life.'

Still gazing through the carriage window, he hears the stranger reply, in a voice that is strangely distant now. 'Perhaps you will have to answer that one yourself, Pilgrim'

There is another long pause.

'No! Ewan MacLeod is wrong stranger, so very wrong; childhood events *do* effect the way one turns out in later life. In my case, the greatest victims were my own dear family - and that was so unfair, so cruel. I can only hope that my treatment of little Angus hasn't perpetrated relationship troubles for him and for his children - and their children even! Know what I mean stranger? How far down the line can the repercussions go on? *The sins of the fathers* and all that. In their later years, when men head up the high hill of old age and look back down over their shoulders, back at their life, some can breathe easy, with a sense of satisfaction at their legacy, with no shame as to their lifetime behaviour. Others of us can only look back with regret and with a broken heart, at a road littered with debris, at a legacy of selfishness, hurt and betrayal - when it is all too late to make amends and atone. And when we do finally vanish into the rarefied high mists, our personal demons will inevitably follow us in.'

Willie gazes at the glass in his hand, still brimming with whisky, a faint wistful smile passing his face.

'But over the last couple of years I have devised a plan, stranger. Perhaps even now it is not too late. I call my plan, the *Bright Light* and the *Big Dream.* In other words, I will make a final supreme effort to atone, to apologise – that is my Bright Light. And having achieved that

I will realise my Big Dream – forgiveness! At last! But I will have to hurry. Time runs out – waits for no man!'

Continuing to stare through the window, he distractedly raises the untouched whisky glass to his lips. Unusually, he takes only a minute sip, his thoughts drifting far away from the train, into the night, far out into Rannoch Moor. In reciting the poem, his voice is barely audible:

> *Because I could not stop for Death,*
>
> *He kindly stopped for me;*
>
> *The carriage held but just ourselves*
>
> *And Immortality . . .*

. . . it was Emily Dickinson composed that poem, stranger'

After several moments it registers with him that there has been no response and he drags his attention from the distant edge of the night, back to the train, to the interior of the carriage.

Tired and apathetic by now, and strangely unperturbed, he sees that the seat opposite him is empty. Beyond it too there is emptiness. Peering around the back of his own seat, he sees the remaining section of the carriage - empty! Yes, the stranger has gone. He glances at his watch which tells him it is exactly one hour since the train had departed Fort William - the exact same time it had been when the stranger had first made his appearance(!) and a cold calmness settles on his spine.

*I think I know who you were, stranger. I think I know who you were.*

Swiveling in his seat and breathing sharply he peers through the window again, just in time to see the same wary herd of deer, standing by the same blasted lone tree of earlier, slipping back beyond view.

*Yes, I do know who you were, stranger! . . . ..*(the clanking of the train can be heard very clearly, seemingly louder all of a sudden)*…..But you are too soon. I' m not quite ready! I have my plan, remember? – the Bright Light and the Big Dream.*

He continues to peer through the window, beads of cold sweat rising on his brow, random but defining episodes from his life beginning to flash through his mind:

- *I've got your wee man! I've got your wee man!* -
- *y'orrite Jimmy?* -
- *Some bush, eh?* –
- *Don't we all hiv oor trubbles, eh Mr Morrison?* –
- *You don't listen, Willie. You just don't listen* –
- *Lift me daddy, lift me! Lift me! Lift me!* –

His thoughts drift to memories of his youngest brother Donnie - the poetic, prematurely dead Donnie. How he had envied the stillness so often present in Donnie's life, having never known the serenity of stillness himself. He had known periodic moments of joy, yes, but never stillness - there had never seemed to be time. Something had always been pursuing him, driving him forever forward towards something dark ahead. And in attempting to counter it, he had conjured his escape world of melodrama - nonstop melodrama - Shakespearean sound and fury. And as a result of it all, two words could sum up what had been the sum total of his adolescent and adult life - emotional exhaustion!

Lately, he has been increasingly feeling mentally and physically drained. His body trembling, he is still merely sipping half heartedly at his whisky as he surveys the world outside the carriage window.

Beyond the passing rattle of the train, he knows there isn't another sound out there in the Rannoch wilderness, other than the muffled rustle of the windblown Highland snow. Inclining his head and squinting upwards, it seems as if the canopy of sky is slowly revolving. In its frosty black depths, millions of stars are shimmering like icicle ends, sliding slowly towards the horizon.

Entranced, he can't free his gaze from these drifting beacons. And little by little he is aware of emptiness and longing struggling in the core of his being. The stars are falling one by one before his eyes and disappearing beyond the distant mountain peaks, and each time they drag him further into to the night.

Breathing softly he has forgotten now the constant running away, the bad conscience, the guilt, the dead weight of innocent victims. After so many years of mad aimless fleeing, it seems as if he has come to a stop at last and his body stops trembling. He presses his forehead harder against the glass, waiting for his racing thoughts and heart to calm down and establish peace, and that yearned-for stillness, within him.

But the eating beast stirs and rears anew - clawing and devouring - hot and wet and treacherous. He clenches his arms around his stomach and slumps forward, his head crashing against the table as he pitches onto the carriage floor, upending the still almost full glass of whisky . . .

'................WILLIE! Are you all right? Willie? Hey! Willie!'

He is aware of being gently shaken and he opens his eyes. The train is stationary, the carriage empty except for himself and the two men standing over him. One of the men has taken hold of his hand. His old friend Ewan MacLeod, has come to the station to pick him up.

'Are you all right Willie?'

He looks up and sees Ewen's and the train conductor's anxious faces.

# EIGHT

The window of the flat is slightly open, a gentle breeze billowing the lace curtains. Outside, traffic is endlessly flowing and Glasgow is growling. It is five days since Willie has been confined to bed. The present day is sunny and fine. Pigeons are cooing romance on a tenement roof somewhere, and the smell of Spring, although still some way off, is already in the air. Ewen MacLeod has made him a cup of tea and is sitting in a chair facing the bed. He is wearing his cheerful face and doing most of the talking.

'Och, you did just grand Willie, just grand man. But how was it you came up with the name Alistair McDonald? That has us flummoxed I must say.'

'Well, it was sergeant McRae started it off with the '45 Rebellion. That seemed to confirm a Gaelic slant to things. The riddles fell broadly into place after that - most of them representing historic Gaelic grievances. The problem was the letters of signature. What the hell did they mean? We felt certain that it was there lay the solution - the characteristic suicidal clues left by a killer. So you think you have a case then?

'Aye, looks promising Willie. An Alistair McDonald. One of the two on the list you brought down with you from Skye. A Skye born third year medical student. Subject to manic depression. Bi-polar. Has had four nervous breakdowns in the last five years. Back and forth on an erratic basis between Skye and his studies in Glasgow. His movements coincide exactly with the times and locations of the murders. We found a notebook at his lodgings - crazy ramblings about the "White Settler *Invader"* and the need for a Gaelic revolt *before it is all too late*. A real fruit cake Willie. Yes indeed, it certainly looks promising. Left-handed too! He is almost certainly our man. He is saying absolutely nothing, but we are working on him.'

'You found a notebook?'

'Aye, you want to read what goes on in this fellow's demented mind. I brought a copy along for you to look at. He wanted to establish a *Gaelic Watch Committee*. No doubt an admirable idea in theory, but his suggested solution to Gaelic grievances is violent retribution, his main target being the *White Settlers,* as he calls them. He maintains that by the year 2000, the White Settlers will not only have outnumbered the Gaels in Scotland, but ultimately will be threatening to outnumber the entire Scottish race... My God Willie, what dangerous lunacy.'

Tired and suddenly disinterested, Willie doesn't respond.

Ewan throws him a quick glance. 'We are a civilised people Willie, and we do, and always must, abide by law and order. A few madmen like this and there is grave trouble ahead. It only takes a few like him. We shouldn't regard this poison lightly. It's endemic of what is happening among minority groups around the world today. Some of the most venomous and mindless violence of our time is the violence of determined minority groups with real, exaggerated or imagined grievances.'

Glancing at Willie again, he falls momentarily silent.

'Anyway Willie, I think we have our man.'

'Ach well, that's a blessing at least.' Willie's voice is becoming distant and distracted.

'A blessing indeed. But the name, Willie? Alistair McDonald? How did you arrive at that at all?'

'Colkitto, Ewan....Colkitto.'

'Colkitto?'

'For goodness sake man, don't you know your Scottish history at all? Colkitto! The giant Gaelic chieftain who rode with Montrose. Lead the Highland army, so often called upon by Montrose. Seven feet tall, they said. A Gaelic hero. Colkitto!'

'Aye?'

'Och, man alive Ewan, Colkitto was a nick-name. Alistair McDonald was Colkitto's given name.......there wouldn't be any more tea in the pot by any chance?'

Seeing the sudden look of wonderment on Ewan's face, Willie laughs.

'At the end of the day, Ewan, things were all solved so simply – no big dramas. Just as well that this shebang we find ourselves in isn't a novel. Just think of the crime fiction aficionados who might have been attracted by the prospect of a serial killer and killings: how short changed they would have now felt, how cheated – perhaps even angry. But it isn't a novel, is it Ewan? We know that. It is all real - very real.'

'It certainly is Willie. It certainly is.'

Laughing, the two men raise their hands in the air and exchange a 'high five'.

Two days later, Willie is looking better but is still confined to his bed. Ewan is again by the bedside, sipping noisily at a cup of tea. When Willie speaks, it is softly - distractedly.

'You search for excuses to justify yourself, but perhaps there are no excuses, no excuses at all . . . and yes, at the end, the demon will follow you in.'

There is a long pause. When he continues it is in the same soft voice.

'My intent, I suppose, was to punish myself . . . but, at the end of the day, it was my loved ones I punished . . . and I drove them all away.'

His cup stationary, halfway to his lips, Ewan regards his friend in silence, realising that he has been speaking largely to himself. After a while, Willie speaks again, but louder and more directly now, at the same time gazing at something far off beyond the window.

'You know Ewan, I had the strangest dream last night. Yes, so very strange. I took Flora, my dear old mother - and her dead now so many years - for a run on my motorbike. On the motorbike! Of all things! It was that motorbike, and the demon drink of course, was the cause of the terrible fallouts we used to have so often in my younger wilder days.' He pauses to smile to himself. 'Although she never reconciled herself to the drink, she came around eventually to the idea of the motorbike. In a mad moment, she even came a wee run on the pillion. Despite all, she had spirit that way.'

There is a new silence and Ewan glances towards him. He is still staring through the window, as if listening to something faint that only he can hear above the growl of the city traffic.

Iain Ferguson

'I took her to see the River Jordan would you believe. Wasn't that the craziest thing? Wasn't that a stupid dream? We rode along a dusty desert road, among giant sand dunes and through sweet smelling orange groves, slow and easy, a warm evening breeze on our faces, mother's auburn hair blowing loose and free. I glanced over my shoulder towards her. She was smiling and had the radiance of a beautiful young woman again. I stopped on a high plateau and pointed below. *Look mother!* I said. *That is the River Jordan.*

*Oh, is that the River Jordan, eh?,* she replied in that soft Highland voice of hers.' He smiles to himself again. 'She had that same habit of rhetorical questions that her younger brother Finlay was to pick up. *Well, well,* she said, *the River Jordan, eh? Och here, isn't it nice Willie, eh?* . . . you know Ewan, when my mother died I never wept for her. It all built up inside me, but it wouldn't spill out. It was as if that by weeping I would be acknowledging that she was gone. I had made my peace with her by that time, you see, but I felt that I still had more making up to do, so I couldn't let her go.'

He continues to stare through the window.

'A very important entity is the mother - for all of us....perhaps the most important entity in one's life. I remember a television programme with an old nurse recalling her experiences on the battle front during World War One, when terribly wounded and dying soldiers were being brought into the field hospitals. They were mostly young lads, but many were grown men. In the face of death, almost all of them would call for their mothers; some of them pleading to hear, for one last time, old songs their mothers used to sing....'

Ewan sips, silently now, at his tea.

'What do you think it meant Ewan, that crazy dream - the symbolism of the motorbike, that symbol of my early defiance?'

'I think you were apologising Willie. Apologising to your mother for all that early trouble you caused her. And from what you just told me, I'm sure you were forgiven; your mother was telling you that everything between you was just fine, not to fret yourself. She understood. There was no more apology needed.'

There is another long pause and Ewan glances again at his friend. Gold from the afternoon sun is reflecting in his eyes, a bubble of liquid appearing in one corner, a bubble that grows steadily fatter . . . trembles . . . breaks loose . . . and slides slowly down his cheek.

Ewan looks quickly away, rises and moves to the window.

A madness of traffic is racing in two directions, heading to God knows where, hell for leather, over the bridge crossing the river - crossing that famous river, The Clyde.

A week later, Willie is back on his feet and pottering around the flat. Two days after that he has a relapse. Ewan anxiously follows the ambulance men carrying the stretcher down the tenement stair. Willie is conscious but Ewan decidedly doesn't like the look of him.

Reaching the ground floor, Willie is aware of somebody pressed against the wall of the close to let them pass. He glances sideways and sees the 'new woman' staring down at him, an expression of concern on her face which she tries to disguise with a tentative smile. As he had decided the very first time he had seen her, she has the sort of warm womanly face he has always liked. And then he becomes aware of a second person behind her - a man. He sees her grab the man's arm in concern as she passes beyond view.

So, she didn't live alone - hadn't been lonely, as he had so often, in his own loneliness, supposed. No sir, she hadn't lived alone or been lonely at all! A bleak and defeated little expression, directed at nowhere, drifts across his face. And the ambulance roof slides above him, obliterating the grey Glasgow sky.

It says one thirty five am on the hospital ward clock, but on account of Willie's deteriorating condition Ewan has been allowed to remain by his bedside. Willie is staring at the ward ceiling and Ewan has fallen awkwardly silent. Eventually Willie speaks, his voice having become a breathless croak.

'The doctors and nurses have been very nice you know. Couldn't have been nicer Ewan.'

'Yes, Willie, they are all very caring people.'

Willie continues to stare at the ceiling.

- *You never listen Willie, you just never listen –*
- *Lift me, daddy! Lift me! –*

'You say you sent word to Sarah and Angus, Ewan? . . . It would be nice if they could come…very nice…. but perhaps they are busy….I hope they come…. I have a plan – a Bright light and a Big Dream . . . .oh yes, I have something to say….so very much to say….but yes, perhaps they are busy….'

Aware of the weakening in Willie's voice, Ewan lifts his friend's hand into his own. 'Och, don't be going fretting yourself Willie. They will come for sure. London and Leeds is a long way, but they will come, have no fear of that. They would have received the telegrams this morning,'

- *You never listen Willie, you just never listen –*
- *Lift me, daddy! Lift me! -*
- *Och, I am tired Angus*

'What a waste of a life Ewan…. what a terrible waste of a life….all that available precious love - squandered!'

Ewan tightens his grip on Willie's hand. 'Willie! . . . Willie! What kind of talk is that! You are in the right place, they will have you up and about before you can blink.'

'Och man, I'm done . . . just run my course altogether . . . I have already met and spoken to Death, Ewan. We met on the train . . . I wasn't afraid . . . I found that rather strange'

There is another awkward silence before Willie continues, as if speaking to himself again.

'You see, it wasn't really me anymore in that body….. I was no longer there….the laughing optimistic young boy, the real me, had been ripped out and replaced by a demon, a frightened and confused demon, perhaps, but a demon for all that - and I could do nothing about it, my life just ran away from me...it was so unjust....more unjust to beloved others than to me....but there still was no excuse for what I did.....'

There is yet another long drawn out silence.

'... and then there were these three little words that I could never bring myself to say - *I love you* ... three simple words that could mean so very much; that had the power to change the world, to make everything just fine - *I love you* ... I was embarrassed and uncomfortable with them.'

Steadily weakening and visibly fading away, Willie smiles faintly. 'Do you know something else, Ewan? Even now, to this day, I have difficulty saying these beautiful words - *I love you.* Isn't that so terribly awful?... But that was the demon again.'

Becoming distraught, Ewan feels a surge of helplessness. He glances at the ward clock - one fifty-four am - and has a sudden remembrance of someone once telling him that the most common time for the dying to die was around two o'clock in the morning.

'Willie, let me say a prayer. Do you mind if I say a prayer?'

Willie swivels his eyes and sees the haunted look in his old friend's face. He smiles and faintly nods, and Ewan gently lifts both of his hands into his own, in a praying attitude before his bowed head.

*'Oh, Dear Merciful Father, forgive us for we have sinned...*

Willie returns his gaze to the ceiling and tells himself: 'There is no Bright Light – no atonement.'

*... and accept us into the Kingdom of Heaven.'*

And he continues to stare at the ward ceiling which slowly dissolves into drifting clouds, the same clouds that his brother Donnie had seen. And he is aware now of himself imperceptibly levitating towards them and of a distraught Ewan squeezing his hand, and he slides a fading glance of fondness towards his old friend, and whispers:

'It doesn't go away, Ewan.'

Attempting a smile, he closes his eyes . . .

**- END -**

Iain Ferguson

*And so the beast - the paedophile - hadn't killed the child, but he had destroyed his soul and stolen his innocence - had prevented him from being how he was meant to be.*

*And now that beast - the paedophile - devious and untroubled as always, moves on - job done! And other vulnerable victims, in abundance and voiceless, await him!*

**For Mags, Coinneach and Fi**

## ABOUT THE AUTHOR

The author was born in Scotland in 1935, in the then notoriously violent Gorbals, an overcrowded slum district in the city of Glasgow. Both his parents were native Gaelic speakers, from the Hebridean island of Skye. With the outbreak of World War Two, it was to Skye that the author was dispatched, as a child evacuee, to the safekeeping of his maternal grandparents. During this formative five-year period, he discovered his roots and established an enduring passion for the Gaelic race, their language and their culture.

Back in Glasgow, the author studied at the Glasgow School of Art.

This was followed by a period of 'restlessness' and general loss of direction. With a view to bringing life back under control, the author then gained entry to Headington College, Oxford, from where he graduated as an architect - at the grand old age of 35! Thereafter, almost all of his architectural career was conducted in the Kingdom of Saudi Arabia.

A lifelong motorcycle enthusiast, he raced several British machines, as an amateur, during the mid/late 1950s.

(The photograph posted below shows him with his Ducati, circa 2014)

Married with a grown-up son and daughter and several grandchildren, the author and his wife currently live in the Scottish West Highlands.

Printed in Great Britain
by Amazon